Good ~~Girls~~ Ghouls Do

Julie Kenner

BERKLEY JAM, NEW YORK

THE BERKLEY PUBLISHING GROUP
Published by the Penguin Group
Penguin Group (USA) Inc.
375 Hudson Street, New York, New York 10014, USA
Penguin Group (Canada), 90 Eglinton Avenue East, Suite 700, Toronto, Ontario M4P 2Y3, Canada
(a division of Pearson Penguin Canada Inc.)
Penguin Books Ltd., 80 Strand, London WC2R 0RL, England
Penguin Group Ireland, 25 St. Stephen's Green, Dublin 2, Ireland (a division of Penguin Books Ltd.)
Penguin Group (Australia), 250 Camberwell Road, Camberwell, Victoria 3124, Australia
(a division of Pearson Australia Group Pty. Ltd.)
Penguin Books India Pvt. Ltd., 11 Community Centre, Panchsheel Park, New Delhi—110 017, India
Penguin Group (NZ), 67 Apollo Drive, Rosedale, North Shore 0745, Auckland, New Zealand
(a division of Pearson New Zealand Ltd.)
Penguin Books (South Africa) (Pty.) Ltd., 24 Sturdee Avenue, Rosebank, Johannesburg 2196,
South Africa

Penguin Books Ltd., Registered Offices: 80 Strand, London WC2R 0RL, England

GOOD GHOULS DO

This book is an original publication of The Berkley Publishing Group.

This is a work of fiction. Names, characters, places, and incidents either are the product of the author's imagination or are used fictitiously, and any resemblance to actual persons, living or dead, business establishments, events, or locales is entirely coincidental. The publisher does not have any control over and does not assume any responsibility for author or third-party websites or their content.

PRINTING HISTORY
Berkley JAM trade paperback / September 2007

Library of Congress Cataloging-in-Publication Data

Kenner, Julie.
  Good ghouls do / Julie Kenner. — Berkley Jam trade pbk. ed.
    p. cm.
  Summary: Sixteen-year-old Beth Frasier, very unhappy about her undead state, must find and kill the person who turned her into a vampire in order to get her life back, but bloodsucking seems to be catching on at Waterloo High and she must watch her back—especially since she turned her boyfriend and his only hope is to kill her.

  ISBN 978-0-425-21703-0
  [1. Vampires—Fiction. 2. Dating (Social customs)—Fiction. 3. Friendship—Fiction. 4. High schools—Fiction. 5. Schools—Fiction.] I. Title.

  PZ7.K3885Gnw 2007
  [Fic]—dc22
                                                                        2007020324

PRINTED IN THE UNITED STATES OF AMERICA

10 9 8 7 6 5 4 3 2 1

Raves for Julie Kenner and her novels!

"What would happen if Buffy the Vampire Slayer got married, moved to the suburbs, and became a stay-at-home mom? [A] sprightly, fast-paced ode to kick-ass housewives . . . Readers will find spunky Kate hard not to root for in spheres both domestic and demonic."
—*Publishers Weekly*

"Great fun; wonderfully clever."

—Jayne Ann Krentz,
New York Times bestselling author

"A fabulously fun heroine . . . [an] ingenious literary creation from Kenner, whose sharp sense of wit is the perfect accessory for this chic blend of chick lit and thriller." —*Booklist*

"It's a hoot."

—Charlaine Harris, *New York Times*
bestselling author of *All Together Dead*

"Smart, fast-paced, unique . . . a blend of sophistication and wit that has you laughing out loud."

—Christine Feehan, *New York
Times* bestselling author of *Dark Celebration*

"Tongue in cheek . . . fast pacing and in-your-face action. Give it a try. Kate's a fun character, and keeps you on the edge of your seat." —SFReader.com

"Ms. Kenner has a style and delivery all her own . . . fun and innovative."
—FallenAngelReviews.com

"You're gonna love this book! Lots of humor and crazy situations and action." —FreshFiction.com

And look for Julie Kenner in
Fendi, Ferragamo, & Fangs
Available now from Berkley JAM!

Prologue

In case you're wondering, there are at least one or two things worse than getting turned into a vampire against your will. Like, for example, turning your boyfriend into a vampire against *his* will. And then hiding out in the school basement while he recovers from the whole human-to-vampire transition thing. And then coming up out of the basement and having some of the gossipiest kids in school see you. And having them realize that you've been down there—in the basement, with a boy—for almost twenty-four hours.

It's one thing to be a vamp. It's another thing altogether to be a vamp with a reputation as a slut.

Maybe I shouldn't have cared what anyone thought. Considering what I'd been through, the rumors that Clayton and I had been doing *it* in the basement were tame compared to the truth—the truth being that he'd almost been killed by a vile, centuries-old vampire who also happened to be the high school's star quarterback. And since he'd only *almost* been killed, I finished the job.

Better a slut than a murderer, right?

Honestly, I wasn't sure. Neither adjective was going to look good on my college applications. But since I was undeniably still dead despite all my attempts to undead my undead-iness, I was thinking that my concern about college was a little bit misplaced.

But I'm getting ahead of myself. My name is Elizabeth Frasier, and I'm set to be the valedictorian of Waterloo High once I'm a senior. I'm also a vampire, and none too happy about it. Sure, the eternal youth thing has some surface allure, but the shiny façade tarnishes real fast. Think about it—sixteen forever? Carded in bars *for the rest of your life*? Who wants that?

The culinary aspects suck, too. Literally. Because, yes, what you've heard about vamps is true. Blood. Anything else and you end up retching your guts out. Translation: no more late night McDonald's drive-bys. No more Häagen-Dazs pig-out sessions with your best friend. No more popcorn at the movies.

Yes, vampirism truly is the torment of the damned.

Worst of all, this whole vampire thing has completely blown my chances of getting into college, much less the film school at Tisch, my Nirvana of higher education. Not that the applications are all that specific, but I think it's a given that the admission board expects an applicant to not only have done reasonably well on her SATs but also be alive.

So, yes, the whole undead thing kind of pissed me off. It's not like I asked to be a vampire. They tricked me. There I was, biding my time until graduation, keeping my grade point average up and spending my spare time editing the school newspaper and trying to figure out what snazzy project I could pull off for this year's science fair. A slightly nerdish existence, maybe, but it worked for me.

In the midst of all that, though, Stephen Wills took a liking to me. Or so I thought.

Hunky, dreamy quarterback Stephen Wills finagled a way for me to audition for cheerleader (which is *so* not like me, but extracurriculars look good on a college transcript, and, hey, it was Stephen-freaking-Wills). But once I got over the raging hormones (which happened about the same time I ended up dead), I realized that Stephen wasn't interested in *me*. He only wanted to get close to me, turn me into a vampire, and give me a great big incentive for figuring out how to interpret an ancient formula for a daywalking potion.

If that sounds about as complicated as all the political mumbo jumbo you read about in world history . . . well, it is. A whole big web of intrigue with me right there at the center.

And, yes, I realize that I should have known better. My only excuse is that my usually sharp brain was operating under the influence of lust. Who wouldn't lust after Stephen? He was gorgeous, he was flirty, and before I knew it, he was plying me with Bloody Marys and nibbling on my neck. The nibbling was real. The Bloody Marys weren't. Or, rather, they were a bit *too* real, especially the "blood" part.

Next thing I knew, I was waking up in a shallow grave, gagging on dirt, and confused as hell. I'm smart, though, so I figured out pretty fast that I'd joined that lovely little fraternity of *vampyr*. After that, I started plotting revenge, and when I learned that I could be restored to human if I killed the vampire who made me, I ramped those efforts up 1,000 percent. After all, the scenario was perfect: kill Stephen, rid the world of one more vampire, get revenge for the dirty trick he played on me, and get my life back.

There was only one problem, and I should have seen it coming. I've watched a billion movies over the course of my life, right? And the best ones always have a twist at the end.

Something unexpected in the third act that turns the plot 180 degrees.

I knew that, and yet I never thought to apply it to my own life.

I should have, though. I'd spent all my free time figuring out how to kill Stephen Wills, but once he was dead, I was still a vampire.

Stephen Wills, it turns out, *didn't* make me. I have no idea whose blood I drank in that fateful Bloody Mary. But unless I find out—unless I kill my real master—I'm going to stay undead forever.

Chapter 1

"But you don't know *who* to kill," Jenny protested, her whispered voice barely audible. We were huddled together at our usual table in the cafeteria, and Jenny was determined to talk about this.

"That's the point," I said, glaring at her. "I need you to help me figure it out."

She leaned back in her chair and eyed me critically, then turned that same intense inspection to the contents of her lunch sack.

"Peanut butter again?" I asked, hoping to distract her.

Jenny shook her head, her expression filled with disgust. "I told Mom that she needed to put a little more consideration into the caloric value of my lunches. Peanut butter is out."

"So what do you have?"

"Sushi," she announced, her face pale. "She's feeding me raw fish. She is *so* punishing me for not making my own lunches."

I laughed. "I love sushi."

She shoved the bag toward me. "Then *you* eat it." A half second later, she pulled the bag back, her face a mask of contrition. "Sorry. I—"

"It's okay," I said, taking a sip of blood from my Waterloo High School sports bottle. One of the many sports bottles I'd taken to carrying around with me, even though I can barely remember the difference between a field goal and a touchdown.

Honestly, though, it wasn't okay. It wasn't okay at all. Because I wanted the sushi. I wanted sushi and pizza and movie popcorn. And unless I found the jerkwad vampire whose blood I'd drunk that very first night, I was never going to be eating those things again.

"We'll find him," Jenny said, reading my mind.

I made a face. "Sorry if I'm not bubbling over with enthusiasm, but I thought I'd taken care of this problem when I . . . you know."

"Whacked Stephen?"

"Shhhhhh!" I slunk down in my chair, quickly checking to make sure no one had overheard. "Are you tripping?"

Jenny just rolled her eyes. "No one has any reason to think we had anything to do with his disappearance."

"That's because no one has any idea at all *why* he disappeared."

"Um, *duh*. He's in California now, remember?"

"I guess." After the whole me-killing-Stephen thing, Chris Freytag had started a rumor that Stephen's dad had been transferred to Los Angeles. One of those sudden things that—*poof*—made the star quarterback suddenly pack up and leave in the middle of his senior year.

Chris is a vamp, too. And although I'd at first thought he'd had it in for me, it turned out that we had a mutual hatred of Stephen. Frankly, I'd have thought Chris would have come up with a more inventive explanation. But since *I'd* been in too much of a state to think about anything—much less what the school would think about the sudden disappearance of the homecoming king—I did appreciate the effort.

A few of us knew the truth, of course. But those of us who did knew the *whole* truth—that Stephen was a vamp, and that he'd been making more vamps on campus.

The rest of the student body was blissfully unaware.

I took another big slurp of my blood. "It really sucks, you know? At least before, I knew who to plan against. This time, I've got nothing. I need to kill my maker, but *how*? I don't even know where to start. It's driving me nuts!" I said the last part *way* too loudly, considering that everyone sitting near us in the caf turned to stare. With my heightened senses (the kind that come from being the subject of gossip, not from being a vampire) I noticed several groups of girls lean in toward each other, then point toward me and whisper.

"Great," I said. "Isn't that just great?"

Jenny cocked her head, started to say something, and then stopped.

"What?" I demanded.

"It's just . . . nothing."

"What?" I repeated.

"Well! You're so moody lately!"

I leaned closer to Jenny. "Under the circumstances, you'd be moody, too."

"Ignore them," she said, rummaging in her backpack and finally coming up victorious with a Milky Way bar.

"What about the caloric value of your lunch?"

"This isn't lunch," she said. "It's a snack." She peeled the wrapper back, bit in, and sank back in her chair with a bliss-filled sigh. I resisted the urge to knock the candy out of her hand.

Okay, maybe Jenny was right; maybe I was a little touchy.

She swallowed and looked at me, one eyebrow raised. "This is going to pass and someone else will be next week's rumor. It's not like you *did* sleep with Clayton, right? You'd tell me. Wouldn't you?"

"We slept," I said, sulkily. "And that's all." Well, not all, but Jenny already knew about the whole turning-Clayton-into-a-vampire thing, and I didn't really care to repeat it.

She took another bite of candy. "There you go. Why do you care what these morons think?"

I didn't know why I cared. All I knew was that I did. I'd spent over twenty-four hours crammed in a janitor's closet, practically drowning in guilt. I shouldn't have done it, but what choice had I had? Do nothing, and Clayton would have died. I couldn't let that happen.

And in one of those ironic twists worthy of an essay question in English lit class, I ended up killing him myself. He'd died, but he hadn't *died*. He was like me. Undead. Stuck in a living hell.

But did anyone care about my heart-wrenching, gut-turning decision? No, they did not. Instead, when Clayton and I emerged from the basement right after sunset, exhausted and rumpled and quite the worse for wear, the few kids still loitering in the halls who saw us jumped to their own nonvampiric conclusions. By the time I got home less than two hours later, I had seventeen e-mails asking me if it was true.

It was almost enough to make me think I was popular, what with that many people speculating about my love life.

Almost, but not quite.

"Do you want me to put something on the blog?" Jenny asked. "Something about how you guys didn't sleep together?"

I shook my head. Jenny is the voice behind the *Waterloo Watch*, a hugely popular blog that posts and comments on the burning gossip of the day at Waterloo High. I, however, am the only one who knows that, since the author of the blog is completely anonymous.

The site had started out as a fun little thing she did, but then it started getting a massive number of hits. Now, there's probably not a student in the school who doesn't visit it at least once a day. "Power of the press," Jenny was always saying, and for the most part, I had to agree with her.

"Don't write anything," I said. "That would only make people think about it more."

"Focus, Beth," Jenny said. "He *is* your boyfriend. People are going to think it anyway."

"One," I said, counting on my fingers. "He's barely my

boyfriend." Sad, but true. We were still in that nascent dating period. That whole getting-to-know-you stage that can be so easily ruined by, oh, one-half of the new couple turning the other half into a vampire. "And two, there isn't a person at this school who thinks about me on a regular basis. Not unless they have a reason to."

"Well, that's true," Jenny agreed, and we both stayed quiet for a second, glorying in the delightful anonymity bestowed by extreme unpopular-ness.

"Except for the barely part," Jenny added after a moment. "*I* think about you. And Clayton is totally into you."

I grunted noncommittally. There are probably statistics about the number of relationships destroyed by unrequested vampire turning, but I didn't intend to be the one to look them up.

Jenny watched my face, her own expression worried. "Do you think he's going to break up with you over the whole blood-sharing thing?" she asked. "Was he acting all weird after he woke up? Because you didn't tell me if he was acting weird."

"He'd just realized he'd been turned into a vampire," I said, unable to keep the exasperation out of my voice. "I think a little weird is to be expected."

"So he was weird?"

"Yes," I said, then frowned. "Or, no. Not really." I looked at her helplessly. "Is it weird that he wasn't weird?"

"No, no, no," she said, but with almost too much sincerity, you know? "Clayton's a cool guy. That's just Clayton being normal." A little V appeared between her eyebrows. "That's what you mean, right? That he seemed cool with . . . you know . . . *everything*?"

"Yeah," I said, remembering back. "He was cool." I frowned. Maybe a little too cool? I'd told him I was sorry, and he'd said it was all right. But he hadn't kissed me. He hadn't done much of anything, really.

Oh, God. I wasn't about to get dumped by the only boyfriend I'd ever had. Was I?

"Is he freaked by the rumors?" Jenny asked. "Is that why he's not here?"

I shook my head slowly, starting to feel a little better as I remembered his reaction. "No. It didn't seem to faze him." Typical guy. *His* reputation could only be improved. "But he's still getting his strength up." While vamps *can* walk around during the day—inside, away from the sun—it takes a lot of caffeine to manage it. And considering Clayton was still getting used to his brand-new, liquid diet, he hadn't wanted to push it. And I hadn't pushed him.

"I told him I'd bring by a few liters after school today.

He's probably already blown through my stash." I learned pretty quickly to keep a cache of blood handy. Fortunately, my dad's a doctor and I have a part-time job at the hospital. I've told people I'm begging and stealing blood as part of a science project, and so far no one's batted an eye.

"Well, there you go. You're already planning on seeing each other again, and he's not trying to avoid you. That's good. And you're taking him food. That's very domestic. Very girlfriendish."

"You think?"

"Absolutely."

"Okay," I said, somewhat reassured. "Okay, then."

"Back to business," Jenny said. "What do you want me to do?"

"I don't know," I admitted. "I have to figure out who made me. Since it wasn't Stephen, I'm all out of ideas. A teacher, maybe?" I tried to picture all the teachers in the school. Were there any I'd never seen outside in the direct sunlight?

"It could be one of the other jocks," Jenny said reasonably. After all, quite a few of the team had joined the ranks of the undead.

"There are too many options. And I need to be sure." I didn't have any compunction about killing off the vamps who'd sucked me into this world, but my willingness wasn't the issue. A vampire can't directly kill anyone equal to or higher than them on the undead family tree. Craftier methods are required—hiring assassins, rigging decapitations, that kind of thing. And valedictorian or no, I didn't think I had it in me to be crafty that many times over.

"Maybe Kevin has an idea," Jenny offered. I'd recently met Kevin, a cute college kid who also happened to be a vampire hunter. He'd let me live because there was still a chance I could be made human. At least, that's what he said. Jenny says he's hot for me.

"I can ask him," I said. Not because *I* was hot for him— I had a boyfriend, after all—but because she was right. Next to the actual vamp population, Kevin probably knew as much about the undead goings-on at Waterloo High as anyone.

"Does Kevin know about Clayton?" Jenny asked.

I rolled my eyes. "God, Jen. We haven't been dating that long, and it's not like I'm spilling my personal life to every cute college guy I meet."

She stared me down. "Guilty much?" she asked, and I immediately blushed. Jenny laughed. "You're allowed to think college guys are hot, even if you're dating a high school boy. It's like the golden rule."

"I don't—" I began, but she held up a hand, effectively cutting me off. "Don't even," she said. "*My* question wasn't about your love life. It was about whether Kevin knows Clayton's a vamp now."

"Oh." I considered that. "I'm not sure. If he doesn't now, he will pretty soon. He's got a pretty strong spidey sense for vampires."

"Will he try to . . . you know?"

I licked my lips, feeling more than a little protective of my boyfriend-turned-vampiric-protégé. "No way," I said, but I was frowning. "He let me live, right? And Clayton hasn't fed on living blood either. So long as Kevin knows that Clayton can still be turned back to human, he won't try to take him out."

Jenny stared at me.

"What?" I demanded.

"Nothing," she said, looking away. "I was just . . . nothing."

Clearly it wasn't nothing, and I pressed the point.

"Honest, Beth," she said. "I was being stupid. Really. No big."

I took a deep breath, because I was pretty sure I knew what she'd been thinking. "Clayton wouldn't kill me," I said.

She cocked her head. "You're sure about that?"

"Duh," I said. "He's my boyfriend, remember?" Which wasn't really an answer at all. A little fact that Jenny picked up on right away. She may not pull straight A's, but Jenny's no slouch. And from the way she was looking at me, I knew she wasn't sharing my confidence level.

"There's no reason for him to kill me," I said. "It makes more sense for him to help me kill *my* master. Then we'll both turn back."

"You're sure?"

"Pretty sure."

"Okay," she said, shrugging slightly. "Then I guess you're safe." She frowned, and I knew what she was thinking. You can't spend every year from preschool to high school with someone and not learn to read their thoughts. And right then, Jenny was wondering what Clayton would do if I couldn't find my maker. Or, if after finding him, I couldn't manage to kill him.

I was wondering the same thing. Clayton loved me and all, but did he love me enough to stay a vampire for all eternity?

I truly didn't know.

Jenny took the last bite of her Milky Way. "Do you want me to go with you? To see Clayton?"

I opened my mouth to protest; I *so* didn't need a bodyguard to go to see my boyfriend. Nothing bad was going to happen to me.

Then I remembered that fateful afternoon when I'd gone to meet Stephen Wills on the football field. I'd told myself then that I was only meeting a boy, and look how that had turned out.

I pushed down the thought and straightened my shoulders, determined not to lose faith in the first boyfriend I'd ever had. "No, thanks," I said firmly. "I'll be fine."

I could only hope that I would be.

Chapter 2

I left the school right after sunset and headed west along Barton Springs Road, watching as the headlights from the evening traffic cut through a winter mist that hung over the city. It wasn't cold—it's rarely cold in Austin before January—but the air was thick, and an eerie haze clung to the light of the streetlamps.

Clayton lived on the other side of the river—not too far from me, actually—but with a stay-at-home mom and a dad who worked from an office in the attic, Clayton's house wasn't a bastion of privacy.

His grandfather, however, lived in a ramshackle trailer in one of the last RV parks inside the city limits. Weirdness was not only tolerated there, it was expected. What's more,

Arvin Greene knew about vampires. He'd been a vampire hunter years before . . . and he was the one who'd told me that I had to kill my maker to become human again.

I shivered. Maybe going to see Clayton wasn't such a great idea. After all, Arvin liked me and all that, but he certainly liked his grandson better. And he'd have his grandson back—and fully human—simply by convincing Clayton to take out little old me.

Yikes.

No, no, no. Clayton wouldn't kill me, no matter what his grandfather said. Clayton knew perfectly well that I was ripe for being cured. And once I was human, Clayton would be, too. At least, I was pretty sure that was the way it worked.

I kept on walking, past the Peter Pan miniature golf course and the McDonald's, forcing myself to think warm, fuzzy Clayton thoughts. Like the way his hair looked like he'd just woken up, even if he'd combed it. Or the way his green eyes sparkled when he laughed. Or the way I sometimes caught him watching me when he didn't realize I was looking.

We'd started out bitter rivals, neck and neck for the valedictorian spot. Or, at least, I'd thought we'd been bitter. Clayton, it turned out, wasn't nearly as jazzed on the whole academia thing as I was. In fact, he was more interested in ridding the school of vampires than he was in worrying about what colleges cared about his almost-equal-to-mine GPA.

First, he'd tried to warn me.

Then, he'd tried to kill me.

And after he realized I could still be redeemed, well, then he tried to kiss me.

I let him, of course. And it really had been all that. I mean, a cute guy with a brain who's also a good kisser? Does it get any better?

Not in my world it doesn't. The only thing that would jazz me more than having a boyfriend in my life was actually having a life. And that, I was working on.

I came to a halt in front of the trailer park, my head filled with Clayton, my lips more than a little tingly from anticipating the kiss I was praying he'd lay on me. A solid kiss that would dispel all these icky thoughts about him dumping me . . . or, worse, killing me.

Obviously, my brain and hormones were fully occupied. Which totally explains why I didn't even see the arrow that whizzed through the air, the sharply whittled point aimed straight for my heart.

Chapter 3

Three important points to make here: (1) I didn't die (again?); (2) I had no clue where the arrow came from; and (3) I owe my life (undeath?) to a burnt orange hearse.

Go Horns!

But I should probably back up. Like I said, I never saw the arrow coming, but I did catch sight of the hearse. Burnt orange happens to be the school color for the University of Texas, and although I will be spending my tuition money at Tisch, I grew up in this town, and as any native Austinite will tell you, you can't see burnt orange and not think "Hook 'Em, Horns." Trust me on that one.

So when I saw a flash of burnt orange a few yards inside

the RV park, my brain took note. And when the synapses fired enough to show me that the vehicle was a hearse—as in, used for carrying dead people—I shifted toward it for a better look. I'm not entirely sure why I did—maybe I wanted to commune with the dead-like-me crowd—but whatever the reason, the impulse saved my life. I'd no sooner bent over than I heard a high-pitched whine and immediately felt a stabbing pain in my chest.

I looked down and saw the wooden arrow sticking out of me—and had it been a few centimeters to the left, I wouldn't have seen anything at all. I'd be dust.

Needless to say, I was a tad freaked out.

Since I didn't have a better plan, I screamed and hit the deck in case my archery-minded enemy was loading up another arrow. I rolled over and peered up, but didn't see anyone out of the ordinary. Not unless you count the hearse's driver, who rolled down his window and peered at me. A scrawny kid, not much older than me, he quirked an eyebrow and asked if I needed any help.

"I'm fine, thank you," I said, climbing slowly to my feet and dusting myself off. I barely noticed him. I was too busy searching the opposite side of the street for an assassin with a crossbow. Either that, or a nearsighted shooter from the archery club.

No one.

"Uh, yeah," the driver drawled, staring pointedly at my chest. "You look fine, all right."

I grabbed hold of the arrow's shaft and broke it off, leaving the wooden point embedded in my chest. The guy stared. I stared back.

Since that didn't seem to be getting us anywhere, I bumped up from stare to snarl. "Go."

He went. Score one for the scary vampire chick. The almost dust, recently impaled, scary vampire chick.

Oh. My. God.

That's when it hit me. *Someone had tried to kill me.* Or, you know, *end* me. Since technically you can't kill someone who's already dead.

Clayton?

A quick chill raced up my spine, and I told myself that I had to consider the possibility. It's one thing to be the nice girl in school—the one who is little miss Pollyanna and always sees the best in everyone. It's something completely different to cross over into the realm where rose-colored glasses actually get you killed. That's not a rosy red tint I was seeing—that was my own blood. And it wasn't pretty.

I'd made it to Arvin Greene's trailer, but I stopped shy of the rickety stairs leading up to his door. Maybe I shouldn't go up. Maybe I should simply—

"You trying to count the stars there, girl? Get your tail up here. You've got some explaining to do."

The owner of said trailer stood in the doorway and stared me down.

"I, um . . ."

"Quit dawdling," he said. "Clayton told me what happened. Now I want to hear it from you."

I processed his words through the subtext center of my brain—the part that you turn on during essay exams when the teacher asks you to discuss the author's "theme" or "motif"—and decided that he really was simply inviting me inside. There was no underlying "step in so that we can stake you" message that I heard.

But even though I've made straight A's on every essay exam in my high school career, I still climbed the stairs carefully and kept my senses sharp. If a wooden stake came out of Arvin's pocket, I intended to be ready.

"Well, get yourself in, youngster," he said, holding the door open for me. I'd been invited in before, so it wasn't necessary, but I appreciated the gesture. Maybe it was all an act, but it was nice to think that I was still welcome even if I did turn his grandson into one of the walking dead.

The trailer had a tiny living area, complete with a battered couch and an upholstered recliner that had seen better days. Not that you could see the upholstery from under the cat hair. On the back, a big yellow tabby squinted at me, eyes narrowed in distrust. (Okay, *maybe* I was being a bit melodramatic, but the cat really was staring at me.)

"So Clayton tells me you turned him."

I looked around, wondering where the boyfriend in question was.

"Speak up, girl."

"Yes, sir," I said, holding my chin high. "He would have died if I hadn't."

Arvin Greene—being no dummy—stared me down.

I cleared my throat. "Well, yeah, *technically*, he's dead now. But how many dead kids do you know who can run home and tell their grandfather what happened to them that night?"

Arvin snorted, which I hoped was suppressed laughter and not an asthmatic attack. "You got a good head on your shoulders there, Elizabeth."

Those shoulders relaxed considerably. "So you're not, you know, mad?"

"The boy's still got a chance of coming back. That's thanks to you. So long as we get him back, I'm not mad. Not too mad, anyway."

I took a step backward, toward the door and escape. "To come back, though. He's got to—"

I cut myself off, unable to finish. Grandpa Arvin had no such qualms.

"Kill you," he said. "Yeah, that's a bit of a rub, isn't it?"

"I need to go," I said, my hand already on the knob.

"Hold up there. You're safe here. For now."

I had the door open, but I stopped. "Yeah? Why?"

"You're taking out your maker, right?"

"That's my plan," I admitted. "Not that I've been over-whelmingly successful so far."

"You do that, you change back to human. Clayton, too."

I swallowed, relief washing over me like warm water. "You're sure? I thought maybe, but I wasn't posit—"

"I'm not sure," he said.

"Oh."

My face must have mirrored my confusion, not to mention my fear, because he put a hand on my arm. "But it makes a hell of a lot of sense," he said softly. "That's got to be the way it works."

"And if it's not?"

He took a deep breath and shook his head sadly. "Well, then, young lady, I think you and I both know what that means."

I plunged my hand up and down in a *Psycho* stabbing motion.

"Right through your heart," he acknowledged. "But I like you, girl," he added, with a friendly pat to my shoulder. "So don't take it personally."

Chapter 4

I couldn't really hold it against Grandpa Arvin for saying that he planned to reciprocate for the way I killed his grandson. I even appreciated the fact that he gave me bonus points for understanding that I had to kill Clayton in order to save him. That shows a real ability of the older generation to understand and listen to us kids.

At least, that's what I told myself as I marched to the small bedroom at the back of the trailer. Technically, it's Arvin's junk room, but Clayton claims it as his own whenever he hangs out at his grandpa's.

I paused outside the door, shifting my weight from foot to foot. I'm not entirely sure what I was nervous about, but I was. I couldn't help it.

"Get on with it," Arvin said. "I want to get back to my show." He'd plopped himself down in the armchair, the remote aimed at the television, an episode of *Cops* frozen on the screen.

"Right," I said, then knocked softly. I heard a grunt that could have been permission to come in, and so I did—then immediately wished I hadn't.

"—have to try again," Clayton was saying, his voice barely a whisper. "But not here. I don't want my grandpa to know I'm doing this, and she totally can't know because then I'll never manage to—" He'd been pacing as he talked, but when he turned and saw me, he stopped dead and his already pale face went even paler. "Beth," he said. And then he snapped his cell phone shut without even saying good-bye.

My stomach roiled, like I'd eaten real food or something, and I felt myself shaking my head, even though I was pretty sure I'd entirely lost my ability to control my body.

Like in slow motion, Clayton shook himself and tossed the phone on the bed. Then he smiled. "Oh, man, it's good to see you. I've been going totally stir-crazy here. And starving, too. I love Gramps and all, but when he was getting on me for having the radio too loud, all I could think about was that he'd be one tasty morsel, you know?" He laughed, the sound awkward. "Not that I'd really—"

"Who were you talking to?" I asked, amazed that my voice even worked. I braced myself, certain he was going to tell me he'd hired an assassin to take me out. Bye-bye, Beth. Nice dating you, but that whole undead thing put a little damper on the romance.

"Huh?" He glanced at the bed, where the phone sat, its shiny silver body catching the light as if blinking a guilty message. "Oh. Nobody."

"Nobody," I repeated. *"Nobody?"*

"Yeah. Nobody important, anyway"

"God, you're a coward," I said.

His gorgeous, guilty green eyes widened. "What's your problem?"

I pressed my lips together, my own eyes stinging with tears I couldn't shed. "Apparently you are," I said. "Here." I tossed him the backpack filled with pints of blood, then yanked the door open. "Bon appétit."

And then I was out the door. He made it to the doorway behind me in about two seconds, but by that time I was already down the hall. Arvin looked up from his show, but I didn't even acknowledge him. "I really thought we—" I began, but then I stopped. Why should I confess warm, fuzzy thoughts to a guy who wanted to kill me? Somehow, that just seemed wrong.

Julie Kenner

So instead I stormed out the door and stomped down the stairs.

I'd had a boyfriend for less than a month. I'd liked the couple thing, and I'd loved him. But now it was over, and all because some idiot vampire had wanted me to make a day-walking formula.

I wished I could still cry, because wallowing seemed like a really good idea right then. But I couldn't. I'd been vamped, and crying had gone the way of eating and walking during the day.

I fisted my hands, thinking of the unknown vamp whose blood I'd drunk. He'd messed with me. He'd messed with my college prep. And he'd messed with my love life.

I was *so* getting revenge.

Chapter 5

"He tried to have you killed?" Jenny screeched, her digitized voice high and tinny. "Oh, man, that is so lame!"

I sighed into the phone and continued my pity party as I walked down Lamar Boulevard toward the river, and toward home.

"I totally didn't expect he'd do anything like that," she said. "It crossed my mind, but I never believed he'd actually . . . I mean, *jeez*, he positively adored you. If he could hire someone to take you out, well, that pretty much puts a big ol' pox on all the males of the species. Or, two species, I guess. I don't know. At any rate, it sucks. Pardon the expression."

She continued on, rambling sympathy and outrage, but it was all rolling off me. After the realization that your boyfriend tried to have you whacked, picking apart the details is blatant masochism, you know?

"—sure? Because you might be wrong."

"I'm sorry. What?"

Jenny sighed. "I said that you might be wrong. Clayton thinks you're the greatest."

"*Thinks* is present tense. You should try past."

"I hate grammar," Jenny said. "And my English grades prove it." Jenny got a B+ last semester in English, and she's still sore about it.

"Regardless," I said, "he was totally setting me up for something . . . to fix something that failed. Like, oh, an attack on my life that happened to fail miserably."

"I guess . . ."

"I'm not guessing," I said, my heart tightening despite the whole nonbeating thing. "I know. He can't kill me himself, remember? But he still has to be the reason I die."

It's a whole big vampire rule thing. A vampire can't kill the vamp who made him. But to become human, he *does* have to get his maker dead—really, really dead. Quite the conundrum, but as Arvin pointed out to me, all that means is that the makee has to set the circumstances in motion to kill the maker.

In other words, do something incredibly clever. And hiring an assassin seemed to fit the bill nicely.

"Want me to come over?" Jenny asked, finally with an appropriate level of best-friend pity in her voice. "We could eat Häagen-Dazs and bitch about boys." And then, "Oh. Sorry."

"Ix-nay on the ice cream," I said. "But it's a nice thought."

"I don't mind," she said. "I can be there in ten."

I wasn't in the mood. "I'm okay. But I want to be alone."

"Right. Sure. And tomorrow's like a whole new day. Trust me," she said. "You'll feel better then. Are you coming to school?"

I really didn't want to. For one, Clayton might be there, and I wasn't up for seeing his smiling face. For another, it's a huge effort to get to school these days, what with having to suck down pint after pint of caffeinated blood. And even then, it's hard to fight the sleepies.

At the same time, though, I'd spent the last few weeks working my butt off to get my life back. Now, I needed to work my butt off to keep my grades up. Because if I *did* get my life back, how stupid would I feel if I'd damaged my perfect GPA in the process? Stellar colleges do not smile upon kids who can't maintain a certain academic standard. Trust me. All the how-to books say so.

By the time I signed off with Jenny, I wasn't feeling any better about the whole Clayton thing. But I was much closer to home. And even though home meant a distracted, workaholic mother who hadn't yet clued in to her daughter's crazy new fascination with the nightlife, it was still home. And I wanted my room. And my bed. And Pongo, the giraffe I'd had for as long as I could remember.

I also wanted the ice cream, but that wasn't going to happen.

Honestly, being undead sucks. Literally.

About the only benefit that I've noticed so far is that I can jog for miles and not get the slightest bit winded. Tonight, though, I wasn't in a hurry, and I'd been leisurely (aka, mopingly) making my way back toward my house. So far, I'd crossed over the river (ironically known as Town Lake, even though it is, in fact, part of the Colorado River. Don't ask me; I didn't name the thing). Then I'd made a left onto Sixth Street, passing up all of my previous favorite haunts such as Waterloo Records (which nowadays sells CDs, of course) and Amy's Ice Cream (which has the best Mexican vanilla ice cream on the planet, of which I intend to partake in gallon-sized doses once I get my life back).

On the whole, Austin is a pretty cool town, and near downtown is a fun place to live. There's all sorts of stuff in walking distance, from stores to Zilker Park to really good restaurants. The town's been featured in *National Geographic*, and it's famous for the humongous colony of Mexican free-tailed bats that live under the Congress Avenue bridge.

All pretty neato-keeno, huh? That's what I used to think. It's my hometown, and I've always liked it. Lately, though, I've discovered a few rather unpleasant facts about the place. Like the fact that it's teeming with teenage vampires. I know the city motto is "Keep Austin Weird," but I think that's taking things a bit too far. And the fact that the vamps have a hefty stronghold at my alma mater—Waterloo High—only makes matters worse. Especially since I'm now one of them.

Not that I have much right to complain. After all, I'm contributing to the vamp population, but still. Had the undead monsters not changed me, I wouldn't have changed Clayton. So forgive me if I was a little touchy about the subject.

I made a right turn and trotted up the hill toward my house. We live in a neighborhood filled with restored 1930-something bungalows, and now that we'd hit the tail end of November, quite a few of the houses were lit up in anticipation of Christmas. My melancholy lifted a teensy bit. Maybe I couldn't go outside during the day, but with my enhanced vision, the holiday lights were more than pretty—they were magical.

The house on our corner always does the lights way up, and this year was no exception. The house dripped white lights, and Santa perched on top, his bag of toys balanced on the back of his sleigh, Rudolph's red nose lifted in welcome.

The rest of the yard was as festive, with a throng of wooden snowmen, fully frozen despite the still-green buffalo grass and the seventy-degree weather so common to central Texas this time of year. One snowman's eyes peered up, as if he was checking out the blinking rainbow of lights that stretched from treetop to treetop, creating a multicolored blanket under the sky.

In truth, it was all a bit too much too early, but I loved it. I had ever since we moved to the neighborhood. And now I crept onto the lawn and lay down, watching the colors above, luminous against velvet-black night. I might never see a sunrise again, but at least I could watch this.

I was still there being all melancholy and sixteen when my phone rang. I snatched it from my purse, hoping the people in the house hadn't heard it, and answered without checking the caller ID. Immediately, I wished I hadn't.

"Are you okay?"

I sat up, Clayton's voice destroying my good mood. "Fine," I said. "Why wouldn't I be?"

I couldn't help the challenge in my voice, and I'm sure he heard it, because his next words were carefully measured, like he was talking to a crazy person or something. "I don't know," he said. "You left so fast. I didn't even get to— Nevermind."

"Didn't get to what?"

"Forget it," he said. "It's no big deal. I just . . ."

His voice was low and edgy, sexy-like, and I shifted, wishing he were right there with me, and at the same time trying hard to remember why I'd run away. Attack. Me. Dead.

All those little details that screw up a budding relationship.

I knew I should hang up and go home. Should ignore him. Instead, I whispered, "Just what?" then cursed myself. Apparently a 4.0 GPA is utterly useless when confronted by teenage hormones.

"You were acting so . . . well . . ." He took a loud, long breath. "It's only that you left without letting me kiss you good-bye."

"Ohhhhh." I suddenly felt tingly all over, and the lights

seemed to blink a bit more in celebration. *I'd been wrong! I'd been an idiot!*

"So?"

"I'm sorry. I didn't mean . . . I thought . . ." I climbed to my feet. "I've been a little moody," I said, my voice bordering on giddy. "It wasn't you. Really." I hugged myself and spun in a circle, a celebratory rant of "he didn't try, he didn't try, he didn't try to kill me" running through my head to the tune of "Jingle Bells."

"Good." A short pause, and then he said, "I could come over. Where are you?"

"Almost home. I'm looking at the lights on the house on the corner."

"Cool," he said. "I'll be right there. Wait for me?"

"Sure," I said, grinning like a fool, and hugging myself so hard I probably bruised my own rib cage. I did a little dance, then spun in a circle, my arms out wide, and my head tilted back so that the lights seemed to make rainbows across the night sky.

Apparently vampirism isn't a cure for dizziness, because after a few minutes of that, I had to lie down again. I spread my arms out, like I was making snow angels in the grass, closed my eyes, and felt the world spin underneath me.

He still loved me.

Wow.

Oh, wow.

I opened my eyes long enough to fumble for my cell phone, hit the speed dial, and let my head drop back on the soft cushion of grass.

"Urgh?" came Jenny's muffled, incoherent response.

"I woke you," I said, stating the obvious.

"That's okay. I was only sleeping." A very loud yawn, then, "What's up?"

"He wanted to kiss me!" I said, way more interested in my love life than in Jenny's lack of sleep.

"Clayton?"

"No, Dracula. Of course, Clayton!"

"Whoa, whoa," she said, and I could hear the rustle of sheets as she propped herself up in bed. "I thought he wanted to kill you."

"So did I." I could feel myself melting even as I thought about it. "But then he said that I was acting strange and, well, you know."

"Actually," she said dryly, "I don't." Jenny had been a long time absent from boyfriend-ville. And while she claimed that her motto was that women only need men to change lightbulbs and carry heavy objects, I happen to know that her uber-feminist rant only goes so far as her next invitation to a dance or the coffee shop.

I gave her the quick yet thorough rundown on my convo with Clayton. "I'm right, right?" I asked, sounding needy but not in the mood to care. "That means he still loves me and wasn't trying to kill me, doesn't it? The whole thing was probably some huge PMS nightmare, right?"

"You still do that? PMS?"

"Um, focus much? That's really not the point."

"But—"

"*No,*" I said, feeling as surly as if I did still do the whole PMS thing. "I'm a vamp. I'm not having a Pamprin moment, okay? Now will you answer my question or what?"

"Sorry. I—"

"AAAAAAAAAAAAHHHHHHHHHHHH!" I screamed and tossed the phone aside as a giant wooden stake came slamming down straight toward my heart.

In my hurry to roll sideways, I didn't get a good look at my attacker, but tall and snarly seemed to fit the bill. And his low growl of "Die, scourge" didn't make me feel any better about the situation, either.

I tried to scramble to my feet, but those damn Christmas lights had me totally disoriented, and my anonymous attacker took advantage, lunging again, so that all I could do was kick and flail and—yes—fight the urge to sink my teeth into his tasty little neck and suck, suck, suck.

That unpleasant reality gave me enough of an adrenaline kick to shove the guy back and get on my feet. Not that it did me any good. Attack Boy had come prepared, and now he took a big stick and started spinning it, like he was Friar Tuck or something.

Apparently Friar Tuck knew what he was doing, because he caught me behind the knees, sending me hurling backward. Even with the preternatural strength that comes from my vampish state, this guy was totally besting me—most probably because I was doing a crap job of defending myself.

From my prone position, I did two things. First, I thrust my arms up in an attempt to keep the wooden stick from serving the same purpose as a wooden stake, and second, I swore to start working out more. Twice in one night was two times too many. And killing my maker wasn't going to do me any good unless I was still among the living. Well, the undead, but you know what I mean.

Considering the way this guy was wailing on me, though, I was beginning to think that I should make peace with moving from undead to dead-dead. I tried to roll aside, but there was a tree in my way. And he was looming above me.

I scooted back, my knees up as I kicked out with my legs, hoping to keep him away, but he kept on coming.

Finally, I pulled a time-honored maneuver—I screamed at the top of my lungs.

The porch light on the house snapped on, but my attacker didn't even slow down. Why would he? In this day and age, most people are too smart to step outside during a fight. They might get shot. They might get bit. Heck, they might even get turned into a vampire.

I squirmed and kicked, trying to land a heel in his crotch, but no luck. With a thundering victory cry, he lunged forward—and then howled in pain.

I tensed, fearing that ear-splitting shriek was my own. After about a second of self-examination and prayerfully patting myself down, I realized that I was still whole.

The same couldn't be said of the giant who'd been hounding me. He'd turned around, and was limping away, the blade of a knife embedded in his thigh.

I blinked in confusion, then saw a tiny bit of movement across the street. I froze, uncertain. Behind me, I heard a voice. "Are you all right, dear?" asked an elderly woman I recognized from years of walking past her as she tended her garden.

I stood up and took stock. "Yeah," I said. "I think I'm

okay." Physically, that is. Emotionally, I was a wreck. Why wouldn't I be? I'd told my potentially homicidal boyfriend exactly where to find me, and the next thing I knew, someone had tried to kill me. True, I didn't know for sure that Clayton was behind the attack. I mean, maybe he was the one who'd thrown the knife and saved me. That was a possibility, right?

Sure, I thought, desperate to convince myself. A definite possibility.

But I hurried home, anyway.

Chapter 6

I arrived home feeling unloved, dejected, foolish and more than a little scared. I'd tried calling Jenny back—so she'd know I still had an un-life—but I only got her voice mail, which left me feeling even more unloved and dejected.

"You could use a little work on your left hook," a disembodied voice on my back porch said.

I jumped a mile, then exhaled in relief as the body in question stepped onto the porch. *Kevin*. His perfect white teeth reflected the moonlight, and his blue eyes twinkled as much as the stars.

Not very long ago, Kevin had almost staked me. That had been a rather unpleasant episode in our friendship, but since he'd let me live in the end—once he realized that I wasn't doomed and could still be turned human again—we were back on solid ground. As solid as we could be with the whole hunter-vamp dynamic working there. Not to mention the college boy/high school girl thing.

"I didn't know I had a left hook," I said.

"Exactly my point."

I made a face and rummaged in my purse for my keys. "*You* threw the knife," I said, the tiny sliver of hope that my savior had been Clayton vanishing with a poof of reality.

"Someone had to save your butt."

I tried to think of something pithy and witty, but nothing sprang to mind. Instead, I resorted to the mundane. "Thanks."

"You're welcome." Kevin is a freshman at the University of Texas. He's tall and blond and as cute as they come. But his status as a vampire hunter puts a little damper on any sparks that there might have been between us. Not that I was looking for sparks. I have a boyfriend, after all. Or maybe *had*—I wasn't sure.

He nodded toward the door. "Can I come in? We should talk."

I started to comply, then shook my head. "My mom's home," I said. This was actually an unusual thing in my family. My mother, home before oh, say, two a.m. In my prevamp days, her late-night hours irritated me. But I'd recently discovered that her hours meshed well with my new nocturnal lifestyle. "I could introduce you, but what would I say?"

Kevin grinned, which made the dimple in his cheek flash. "You could tell her I'm your friendly neighborhood vampire hunter."

"I'm thinking no."

He held out his hands, as if putting himself on display. "So introduce me as your boyfriend."

"She'd know I was lying. She's already met my boyfriend."

"Clayton," he said with a knowing nod. "Right."

I tilted my head, so not wanting to discuss my boyfriend woes with a cute college freshman. Or, for that matter, with a vampire hunter. "What?"

He looked back at me, eyes wide. "What, what?"

"There was a tone in your voice." I squinted at him. "Why the tone?"

"Beth," he said, in that irritating I'm-older-and-smarter voice. "There was no tone."

I totally disagreed about the tone thing, but I wasn't in the mood to argue. "Fine," I said. "But we stay here." My mom's bedroom is in the front of the house. With any luck, we could have a conversation on the back porch and she'd never be the wiser. Plus, I really wasn't allowed to invite friends inside that my mother had never met. And while I *could* drag her out to meet Kevin, the odds were that she was either already asleep because she had to catch some incredibly early plane to go some incredibly boring place to take somebody's incredibly dull deposition. Or, she was locked in her room writing an incredibly dull brief, and if I interrupted her train of thought I'd never hear the end of it.

Best to avoid Mom in the after-dinner hours, when she was home. That's my motto.

"Fine," Kevin said. "We stay here. What I have to say won't take too long."

"What do you have to say?"

"That you're an idiot if you think Clayton's your boyfriend anymore."

I should have been stung by the force of his words. I wasn't, though. I'd already passed idiot and was well on the way to anger, hurt, rejection, and fear. After all, rocket science really wasn't required to put the pieces together.

Still, Clayton was (had been?) *my* boyfriend, which meant that all accusations of badness had to come from me. Accuse my evil, scum-sucking, homicidal boyfriend of trying to take me out, and you darn sure better be prepared to defend the position.

"Oh?" I said, raising a haughty eyebrow. "And what do you know about it?"

"Only that he tried to kill you."

"How did you know?"

"I was coming to see you," he said. "And I overheard your phone conversations. And then our big friend showed up, and . . ."

"Oh."

"I'm sorry, Beth," he said.

I looked down at the porch. "No, you're not. He's a vampire. You kill vampires. It's what you do."

He hooked a finger under my chin and tilted it up. "I haven't killed you."

"That's because I'm still redeemable." Not that I knew who my maker was, but like Jenny had said, Kevin might be able to help me figure that out.

"Well, yes. That and the fact that you're cute."

"About that redeemable thing," I began. "Maybe you could—" I cut myself off as his words penetrated my overly thick skull. "You think I'm cute?"

"Very cute." He leaned in closer, and my heart would have started beating faster, if I'd had a heart to beat. "Very, very cute."

And then he kissed me. An actual, real, honest-to-goodness

kiss that had my insides going all soft and gooey and my body temperature rising. Metaphorically, at least, since I'm pretty sure I no longer had a body temperature.

After a second he pulled away, his eyes stormy and filled with questions. "Okay?"

"I, um, what?" I was having a hard time swimming into reality-land.

"Was it okay that I kissed you?"

"I, um . . ." *Argh.* Could I *be* any geekier? I took a deep breath. "Sure. I mean, no. I mean, I've got a boyfriend and all, and . . ." I trailed off in a lame shrug, feeling way more miserable than a sixteen-year-old girl should feel after being kissed by a cute college boy.

"I think your boyfriend has things on his mind other than romance," he said, stroking my cheek. "But you're right. I shouldn't have kissed you."

"You—you shouldn't have?"

He shook his head. "I'm in college. You're in high school."

I lifted my chin. "I'm very mature for my age."

He laughed. "Yes, you are. That's partly why I . . . well, you know. But I *am* older than you."

I squinted at him. I'd always assumed he was a freshman, but—"Oh, gosh. Are you a senior?"

"Freshman," he said.

I laughed. "So, like, what? You're nineteen? Big deal. My dad's five years older than my mom." *Why* was I arguing this point. I didn't want to date him. I wanted to date Clayton. A nonevil, nonkilling version of Clayton. Didn't I?

"See what I mean?" he asked, smiling. "You're clever. But it's not the age thing."

"Then what?"

"This wasn't the time. Not right now, when you've just found out that your boyfriend is . . ." He trailed off, spinning his hand as if conjuring words. "Let's say he's being less than friendly to you."

"Oh. Right."

"You're vulnerable," he said, edging in closer and making me go all squishy. He hooked his arm around my waist and pulled me close, his breath tickling my ear as he spoke. "I shouldn't be here when you're vulnerable."

"Why *are* you here?"

"What?"

I motioned to the house. "You said you were coming to see me when you overheard my calls. Okay, fine. But why were you coming in the first place?"

His eyes softened, and his mouth curved into a smile. Then he pressed a soft finger against my lips. "To see you."

Oh. Wow. I summoned all my mental energy not to spontaneously combust on the spot.

Kevin grinned, looking pretty self-satisfied. Then he kissed my forehead. "Go inside," he said. "You'll be safe there."

"From Clayton?" I asked. "Or from you?" I gave myself points for sounding daring and sophisticated when I really was about to melt into a puddle of teenage goo.

"Both," he said. He turned and stepped away, then looked back over his shoulder. "And Beth? Don't invite strangers into your house, okay? For that matter, don't even invite friends."

I must have looked blank, because the corner of his mouth lifted and he shrugged.

"It sounds cliché," he said. "But trust no one."

Chapter 7

"**B**ut you trust me, right?" Jenny asked, leaning forward across the battered cafeteria table. All around us, banners decorated the walls, advertising the upcoming Winter Dance. During my freshman and sophomore years I hadn't even noticed those stupid banners. This year, though, I was totally noticing. What was the point of having a boyfriend if you couldn't dance?

Except I didn't have a boyfriend. Or, technically I did, but the whole trying-to-kill-me thing might make date conversation with Clayton a little awkward.

And Kevin didn't count. For one, he wasn't officially my boyfriend since my mother would have a cow if I dated a college boy. For another, despite all his flirting with me the

night before, in the well-curtained light of day, I really had
no idea where I stood with him. Probably a whiny, girly, insecure teenage girl way to feel, but at the end of the day, I
was a whiny, girly, insecure teenage girl. At least where boys
were concerned.

"Earth to Beth!"

I jumped in my seat. "What?"

"I was asking about what Kevin said. You still trust *me*,
right? I can still come over after school, can't I?"

I took a long sip of my Vivarin-spiked blood (cleverly hidden today in a Dallas Cowboys sports bottle) and nodded. "If
I have to stop trusting you," I said, "I might as well stake myself."

Jenny made a face, but otherwise ignored my melodramatic
mood. "So what did Kevin have to say about the maker thing?"

"Huh?"

"You were going to ask him," she reminded me. "You
know. About whether he has any idea who your maker
might be."

"Oh. Right." I cleared my throat. "I, um, sort of forgot to
ask." Which was another way of saying I'd been distracted
by smooches.

From the look she gave me, I could tell that Jenny understood perfectly. My cheeks burned, and she laughed.

"Jenny!" I said, and she deferred my indignation by hastily taking a bite of her turkey and cheese sandwich, thereby earning her an envious stare.

"Sorry!" she said. "But it is my lunch."

"I know." I took another drag of blood, happy at least to be off the subject of Kevin smooches. "I'm sick of this whole vampire thing. I'm dead tired of having a liquid diet. And I'm positively dying for solid food."

Her lips twitched.

"Shut up," I said grumpily, before she could make some bad joke about my "dead tired" and "dying" comments.

"I didn't say anything," she said, way too innocently.

I made a face and took another sip. "Really not in a jokey mood, okay?"

"Right," she said contritely. "Sorry."

"It's just . . . how could he?"

"Which one?"

I blinked at her. "Which one, what?"

"Which guy are you talking about? Kevin kissing you? Or Clayton trying to kill you?"

"*Duh*. The kill thing is way more major. Boyfriend-induced attempted homicide always trumps teenage lust. Seriously. It's in the handbook."

"See?" she said. "You're doing okay." She reached out and squeezed my fingers sympathetically. "You're making jokes."

"Gallows humor," I said dryly.

"So what are you going to do?"

I shrugged. "Same old, same old. School. Studying. Trying to figure out who my master vampire is. The usual."

"What about the formula?"

I frowned. Stephen Wills had insisted that I try to interpret some ancient manuscript that supposedly held the secret to vampires walking around during the day. I'd made next to no progress, thus solidifying my decision to go into the arts and not follow my dad into medicine or research despite my stellar math and science grades.

"Stephen's gone," I said simply. "It's not my problem anymore."

"You don't want to be able to go outside during the day and not fry?"

I'd recently seen the result of fryage on a vampire, and trust me when I say it isn't pretty.

"Of course I do! And if I can figure out which vampire made me, then I'll be on my way to walking outside *and* eating hamburgers. Not to mention having a seventeenth birthday and growing old enough to drink."

"Point taken," she said. "So what do you want me to do?"

"Two things," I said, leaning back in my chair and making this up as I went. "First, pull all the yearbooks for the last four years. And also comb through the file boxes of photos from this year and at least two or three years back, too."

"Okay," she said, but I could hear the bafflement in her voice. "Am I the new photo editor for the paper?"

"The *Liberator*'s not exactly my top priority, you know?" I'm the editor, and Jenny writes a weekly column. But even though I've been working on the Christmas issue in my spare time—as in, during the early morning, predawn hours when I've snuck into the school so as to not have to go outside while it's sunny—I'll have to admit that I've fallen rather behind on my journalistic duties.

"So what am I doing with the photos?" Jenny asked.

"You're writing a column about the last four years," I said. "At least, that's what you'll tell Ms. Shelby if she asks."

"But I'm not really writing a column . . . am I?"

I shrugged. "You can if you want. Got anything planned for next week's issue?"

She gave me *the look*. "Beth. Tell me what you want me to do."

"I figure the vamp who made me has to be in the school. Stephen was working for him, right? And that means the other jocks were, too."

"Or else they were all working for Stephen, and thought he was the head honcho vamp, the same way you did."

"True," I said, then frowned. "But even so, it makes sense that the head dude is in the school. He probably put Stephen in charge of getting the formula in the first place."

"Wow," Jenny said. "It's like a spy thriller. Everyone with a different motive, and you don't know who to trust. Except me," she added, holding up her hands. "You can totally trust me."

I laughed. "I know. That's why I'm trusting you with Operation Daylight Exposure."

"Come again?"

"The pictures," I explained. "I want you to look through them all and make a list of all the teachers and staff. Students, too. Anyone you can't find an outdoor picture of could be my maker."

"Um, okay. But . . ."

"But what?"

"Vamps don't photograph at all."

I rolled my eyes, then dug in my purse for a mirror. I pulled it out, then looked into it, seeing my reflection as clear as a bell. "And I took a Polaroid of myself, too, right after I changed. Just to be sure."

"You're sure it's not because you can still be turned back to human?"

"I'm sure," I said. "I asked Clayton's grandfather. All that stuff's a myth."

"In that case, it's a brilliant plan," she said. "You're so totally smart."

"That's what they tell me," I said. "Smart, but not lucky."

She made a face. "Can't have everything."

"Maybe not," I said. "But I can try." I looked up, saw one of the Winter Dance banners, and stifled the urge to jump up, rip it down, and shred it into a million pieces.

Stupid Stephen Wills. And Stupid Unknown Maker Vampire.

Was it really so much to ask to have a normal teenage life? Apparently, the answer to that was yes, because so far, normalcy had completely eluded me.

"What was the other thing?" Jenny asked, interrupting my slide into nonhappy thoughts. "You said there were two things I could do."

I shrugged, feeling a little silly. "I was thinking about the blog," I admitted. "Using it to help us figure out who's the big baddie."

"How?"

"Beats me. It's your blog. I'm only the idea girl."

She pursed her lips, considering. "I'll think of something. Meanwhile, you should probably know that you're totally dropping in the polls."

"Huh?"

"The Voice of Waterloo poll," she said in a *duh* voice.

"Oh," I said. "Really not too concerned about that at the moment." The Voice of Waterloo is a schoolwide contest to pick a student to represent Waterloo on one of the local TV news stations. All the schools get to send one kid to be an on-the-air commentator. The *Waterloo Watch* has nothing official to do with the voting, but as soon as the contest was announced, Jenny set up an online poll. Probably 85 percent of the student population logs on to vote . . . and to watch the frontrunners' popularity wax and wane.

Tamara McKnight had been way high in the polls, but she'd been knocked down a peg or two recently thanks to my humble efforts to get revenge for her part in making me a vampire.

In addition to being Waterloo High's head cheerleader, Tamara is also Waterloo's number one bitch. On top of that, she's Stephen Wills former girlfriend (and very most definitely not a member of the Beth Frasier fan club). She's not a vamp herself, but she went out of her way to help the jock vamps do whatever it is that jock vamps do.

I'd also learned that she and the other cheer-heads—and this is the yuck part—were not only sucking face with their vamp boyfriends, they were sucking their blood. Because drinking vamp blood makes a mortal stronger. And, gosh, ya gotta do good at cheerleader camp, right?

Honestly. What a world!

At any rate, Tamara had been jamming to win the Voice vote, but her poll numbers had started falling. Apparently mine had, too, but although Tamara cared, I *so* didn't.

Jenny cleared her throat. "There's more," she said. "All the comments about why you're not getting votes are talking about . . . you know."

"Actually, I don't know."

"The thing with Clayton."

"They know I turned him into a vamp!" I was flabbergasted. How could they?

She rolled her eyes. "Not *that* thing. The basement thing. And the . . . you know." This time she punctuated "you know" with a bit of squirming in her chair. "Smooches," she said. "And more."

I let me head fall back as I looked up at the ceiling and groaned. "But we didn't *do* anything!"

"You were locked together in a dark room for over a day. In high school, that's more than enough. Besides," she said, "Tamara's been saying you two were all over each other before getting locked in."

"She what?!" I was so going to kill Tamara.

"Technically it's true," Jenny said. "You were all over him."

"Trying to save his life," I said, leaving out the part about also killing him. "Tamara's just mad at me about Stephen. And the fact that I punched her in the face."

"Tamara's an idiot," Jenny said. "Don't worry about what she says. The important thing is that we can get you up in the polls again."

I rolled my eyes. "Jenn," I said, "I don't want to be the Voice of Waterloo. Put me on television, and I'd totally freak!"

"Not if you rehearse," she said. "And you'd be so much better than—"

I grabbed her arm, and she shut up, turning to look in the direction I was staring. I could tell when she saw him from the sharp intake of breath. Clayton, standing in the doorway, and looking right at us.

"You should go talk to him," she said, and for a half second I was actually grateful to see him. At least she was dropping the Voice of Waterloo topic. "He wouldn't do anything. Not here. Not in the caf."

I glared at her. "Um, hello? He tried to *kill* me." Okay, yes, maybe I should have gone and talked to him. But romantic betrayal can really open a chasm between a boy and a girl, and right then I wasn't much in the mood to build a bridge, you know? I lifted my chin, determined to sound like the voice of reason, *not* the voice of desperate, pitiful emotion. "I don't really have a lot to say to the boy."

"Yeah, but . . . but . . ."

"But what?" I asked, cocking my head.

"Maybe he didn't really mean it."

"Jenny . . ."

"Well, you're the one who said all that stuff about his grandfather pushing him. Maybe he didn't want to, but—"

I held up a hand. "If he didn't want to," I said, "then he shouldn't have. And it doesn't matter anyway." I nodded toward the doorway. "He's already gone."

"Maybe he didn't see you," Jenny said, her voice overflowing with sympathy.

"He saw me," I said. "He definitely saw me."

Good Ghouls Do

I took a deep breath and tilted my head so that the nearest poster for the Winter Dance completely filled my vision. I wouldn't be going this year. Either that, or I'd be going alone.

Chapter 8

I totally zoned out during Latin class. Not a hard thing to do, actually, since the teacher—Mr. Tucker—has a completely monotone voice. And while none of my teachers are as entertaining as, oh, watching grass grow, Mr. Tucker is particularly dull. Plus, I'm pretty sure that he learned Latin back when it was a spoken language.

All of which is to say that it's easy to tune him out. Normally, I'm attention girl. I actually like Latin, and I'm good at it. But today I had other things on my mind.

Which is why I was still sitting there after the bell rang, my mind whirring with various boyfriend/vampire/reputation woes.

"Elizabeth?"

"Huh? What? Huh?" My head jerked up and I found myself in an empty classroom, face-to-face with Mr. Tucker. "Oh. Gosh." I slid out of my chair and started to gather my books. "I'm really sorry. I didn't get a lot of sleep last night, and I guess my mind was wandering."

He waved away my apology. "I'm not worried about your ability to keep up with the assignments," he said. "But I did want to take this opportunity to speak with you."

"Oh. Sure. Shoot."

"Picture this," he said, his face as animated as I'd ever seen it. "You. The state competition. And an ancient text." He grinned at me. "What do you think?"

"Gee," I said. "Intriguing?" Or not, but I knew better than to tell a teacher that I was less than enthusiastic about his passion.

"I knew you'd think so," he said, parking himself on the desk in front of mine. "We'd need to start drilling soon—and get you registered—but considering your level of competence already, I don't see any problem with you competing at the district level in February."

"Oh. February, huh?"

"Is that a problem?"

I thought about the fact that I was ditching cheerleading, and the hole that would leave in my transcript. Latin wasn't exactly what I was shooting for—I pretty much had academia covered—but I did need to have some extracurriculars this year. A big blank spot on my transcript wouldn't look good to the college types. Of that much, I was certain.

"What kind of competition is this, exactly?"

"It's a bit like extemporaneous speaking," he said. "Only you're not speaking, you're translating."

"Oh." I frowned. "I don't get it."

"The participants are each given an ancient Latin text. The competition is timed, and points are awarded for completeness, accuracy, and idiomatic correctness."

I shook my head. "Not sure I'm your girl, Mr. Tucker. I pretty much suck at translating ancient texts."

He stared at me as if I was actually speaking in Latin. "Elizabeth, forgive my curiosity, but what the devil are you talking about?"

"Oh. Ah." Oopsie. Probably shouldn't have opened the door to this conversation. "It's just that I was trying to translate a really old Latin text recently," I said, resorting to being as vague as possible since I could hardly tell him about the daywalking formula. "And I didn't exactly blow right through it." In fact, I'd proceeded at such a snail's pace that Clayton's grandpa had to finish the thing for me.

"I see," he said, his expression suggesting that he didn't

see at all. "Despite that, I still maintain complete confidence in you. You can hardly be expected to do such translations off the top of your head with no practice. It is the drills that we will do—every day after school—that will give you the competitive edge."

"Every day after school," I repeated, hoping I didn't sound as freaked by the possibility as I felt. "I'm going to have to do some rearranging, you know? Can I, um, get back to you?"

"Of course. But don't take too long. February will be here before you know it."

"Right. Sure. No problem." Every day after school sounded painful. But I did need the transcript padding. Talk about a conundrum!

"So tell me, what exactly were you trying to translate?"

I waved the question away. "Some old thing I found in a thrift store. You know. It caught my eye."

"And you were unable to translate it? You shouldn't give up so soon. There is both power and pride in completion. In knowing that a task has been conquered."

I shrugged. "Yeah, well. It's a moot point now. Someone else helped me translate it."

His eyebrows raised. "Indeed. And was the text as fascinating as the quest?"

"Not hardly," I said, thinking about the puzzle-like translation of the formula. "In fact, I'm sorry I even started in the first place. It turned out to be a riddle, and the whole thing is way, way, way more trouble than it's worth."

"I see," he said. "Don't you want to solve the riddle?"

"Not anymore," I said. "I've got other priorities." I smiled at him, determined to get off this subject before I said too much. "But, hey, I guess that's good news for you."

He looked a bit taken aback by that. "How so?"

"Since I'm not solving ancient riddles, I have time for your Latin competition. So," I added, bending down to pick up my books. "When do we start?"

Chapter 9

I *diot*. Idiot, idiot, idiot.

I was *such* an idiot!

I had no one to blame but myself for agreeing to Tucker's Latin competition—I'd only said yes so that we could end that conversation! And as I headed toward my locker, I ran through various scenarios in my head, wondering how best to get out of this new and unwelcome commitment.

Because although the competition did sound kind of intriguing (in a geeky valedictorian sort of way) there was no way I could commit to doing it. School competitions often take place during the day—arrived at via a van full of students all of whom had waited in the blaring sun in a parking lot for thirty full minutes because the van was always late arriving.

Not something I could do. For that matter, not something I wanted to do even if I wasn't a vampire.

To make matters worse, the liter of blood I'd scarfed down during lunch had worn off. I had a severe case of the sleepies and desperately needed another hit of caffeinated blood.

Even the way that my mind was whirring about the whole Clayton-formula-Latin thing couldn't keep my eyes from drooping, and I yawned as I turned into the bank of lockers where my stuff lived.

And then I stopped cold.

Someone had written *Fast and Loose* in red Magic Marker all over the outside of my locker. Someone else had scrawled *h-h-h-hot*. And the final straw was a photograph of me with Clayton, and taped under that the caption *basement buddies, kiss kiss, bang bang*.

I slammed my hand against my locker, my cheeks burning as the seven or eight other kids at their lockers pointed and whispered. Right at the moment, I desperately wished that vampires couldn't blush, because my cheeks were so hot that I was pretty sure the school would burn down if I leaned against anything flammable.

And, yes, I know that in the grand scheme of things what was written on my locker could have been a *lot* worse. But no one had ever done anything like this to me before. I'm the girl that everyone ignores because she's—nice. To now be so blatantly *un*-ignored was more than a little freaky. Especially since everyone was thinking *those* kinds of thoughts about me and Clayton, even though we hadn't done *those* kinds of things.

"It's a good photo, Beth," said someone in a letter jacket I didn't know. "Maybe you should run it in the next issue of the paper."

"Shut up," I said, then focused on opening my locker.

"Yes, Tommy," a familiar voice said. "Why don't you shut up?"

I turned around and saw Tamara staring imperiously down at the crowd. Tommy—aka letter jacket boy—grumbled a bit, but he shut up. And then he left, the rest of the kids trailing behind him.

"Thanks," I said. I wasn't thrilled about being indebted to Tamara, but I wasn't ungrateful, either.

Beside her, Nelson Fuller shifted, his arms crossed over his chest. "Not like we were interested in doing you some big favor," he said. "But we need to talk to you."

"Joy," I said, trying to decide which was better: Tamara and jock-vamp boy, or the mortal cretins who'd skedaddled when Queen Tam had said boo. "Too bad I'm late for class,"

I added. I grabbed the last sports bottle from my locker, then slammed it shut and tried to step away.

Tamara reached out her hand and pressed it against the lockers, effectively barring my way. I stepped to the right, and Nelson did the same thing. Great. I was trapped in a bank of lockers with the Princess of Puke and her new pasty-faced boyfriend.

"Congratulations," I said, summoning my most simpering smile. "You two make such a cute couple."

Tamara's smile froze, and her stare was just as frosty. She gripped Nelson's arm and leaned her head on his shoulder, ramping the simper factor of her smile up about 1,000 percent. "Nelson is wonderful," she said. "He's everything a girl could want," she cooed, while Nelson—too much of an idiot to know when a girl is lying through her teeth—basked in her praise. "But that doesn't mean I'm going to forgive you for killing Stephen. Nelson may be the boy of my dreams, but Stephen *was* my boyfriend, and he deserves my loyalty."

"And I can tell how loyal you've been, Tam. It's been, what? Barely a week since Stephen vanished in a puff? Was it hard to suffer through such a long period of mourning."

The ice in her face turned to fire. "You listen to me, you stuck-up little geek *loser*. Don't think you get to walk away from all this. You're in it, Beth. You're in up to your eyeballs."

"I am *done*," I said, taking a step toward her. "I didn't ask for this. I don't want it, and I'm not interested in playing anymore."

"No?" That came from Nelson. "Well, maybe what you want doesn't much matter. Because we want the formula. And as much as it makes me want to puke, that means we want you."

"You mean you need me," I snapped back. "But I don't need you." I tossed my hair, a much less effective maneuver than the one Tamara had down, but I still think I made my point. "Stephen's dead, Nelson. In case you didn't notice, I got out from under his thumb. It. Is. Over."

Nelson smiled. And I have to say, I didn't like the look of that smile at all. "Oh no, Beth," he said. "It's not over by a long shot."

I shivered a little despite myself and hoped that neither one of them noticed.

"Stephen wasn't the only one who wanted the formula," Tamara said. "You know that."

At that, I laughed out loud. I really couldn't help it. "*You?* Oh, come on! You want the formula so you can become a vampire, walk around during the day, and be acrobat enough to win a damn cheerleading competition. Give me a break. I'm not going to bust my tail in the science lab so you and Stacy and the others can be rah-rah girls."

"You're a cheerleader, too," she said. "I'd have thought you'd show a little more pride."

"I'm out of that," I said. "Been there. Cheered that. Done."

"Your transcript?" she asked, her eyebrow raised. "I thought you needed all those educationally challenged activities to round out your ultra-dull transcript and trick all the colleges into thinking that maybe you have a personality."

I pressed my lips tight together, reminding myself that I couldn't bite her in the neck and drain the life out of her, no matter how much I might want to. And boy did I want to! Mostly, because she was right. I had joined the cheerleading squad to pump up my transcript. I would have been perfectly happy with the drill team, though. It was Stephen Wills—along with help from Tamara and her little clique of Stepford Teens—that had convinced me to dump my pep squad ambitions for the rah-rah world of leading the crowd to cheer.

With Stephen dead, I'd pretty much decided to abandon the effort.

"You can't quit," Tamara said. "You know you can't walk away from this."

"No?" I said, getting my face as close to hers as I could without gagging. "Watch me." Then I pushed her arm off Nelson's and barreled between them and out into the hall. I headed for the journalism room, my legs on autopilot and my head spinning. I'd just defied the queen of the school and lived to tell about it.

All in all, this vamp thing was doing wonders for my self-esteem.

It wasn't until I was well away from them and had slowed my pace to a reasonable crawl that I realized something. Tamara had said I couldn't quit. But quit what? Cheerleading? Or looking for the formula?

I didn't know. But at the moment, I wasn't inclined to go back and ask. I'd won this round. No sense tainting my victory by letting Tamara see that I was a little clueless about the details of my ultimate triumph.

Chapter 10

I walked home after dark, turning down Jenny's offer to drive me. I was in a lousy mood, and I wanted to be alone.

Unfortunately, I didn't think that I *was* alone, and it occurred to me a bit too late that perhaps a ride would have been a good thing. By myself, I was a walking target for Clayton's assassin.

I told myself I wasn't scared. After all, it might be dark, but it was still early. And the streets were crowded with cars and pedestrians. What self-respecting assassin would attack me under those circumstances?

I didn't know, but the way my spidey sense was tingling, I had a feeling I was about to find out.

I made a sharp left into the alley behind the building, tensed, and then heard those footsteps still behind me.

No way, Jose.

I spun around, shifting into defensive mode. Without even stopping to think, I caught my stalker by the neck and thrust backward, my hand tightening on soft flesh. I didn't let up until I heard the metallic clang of a body hitting the Dumpster . . . then I jumped back, immediately letting go, suddenly realizing what I'd done.

In front of me, Elise Lackland coughed and choked, her hands going to rub her undoubtedly sore neck. She sank down on her haunches and stared up at me as if I were some sort of monster she'd met in a dark alley. Technically, I guess I was.

"Elise!" I yelped. "I'm so sorry. I didn't mean—"

"Man, Beth," she said in a really raspy voice, "what's your damage?"

"I've been . . . someone's trying to . . ." I shook my head, giving up on finding a way to answer that with any semblance of the truth. "I've been having stalker dreams. I guess I'm a little edgy."

"And strong," she said. "Working out much?"

I lifted a shoulder. "I started classes," I said, my tone rising as if I were asking a question. "You know. Self-defense?"

"It's working."

"Were you looking for me?" I asked, hoping we could move on to the changing-the-subject part of the conversation.

"I wanted to say thanks."

"Okay. You're welcome." I squinted at her. "What are you thanking me for?"

Her cheeks started to turn pink, and I knew the answer even before she said it.

"Chris," I said. "You guys are back together?"

She nodded, the blush shifting into a more glowing tone. "He said that he'd talked to you. And that gave him the courage to call me again." She looked down at her shoes. "So thanks."

"And you guys are good?"

"Oh, yeah. We're great. It's not totally like before. He doesn't walk me to school in the morning anymore, but that's because the assistant coach has the team working out in the gym way before the sun's even up. Honest, it's absurd how much they work out, especially now that football season is essentially over."

I was starting to get that vacant feeling in the pit of my stomach. "So did he tell you about—"

"Stacy?" She nodded vigorously. "I totally forgave him. A guy makes the football team, and sometimes he changes."

"Isn't that the truth," I muttered.

"So he was going through a phase. And he dated that skank, but he didn't really like her. He told me so." She looked at me, as if for confirmation of Stacy's skankiness. I happily complied with a nod.

"But it's not a phase," I said.

She waved my words away. "I know. He's still on the team. He's going to be totally tempted by cheerleaders and girls who wear makeup better than I do and fit into a size six instead of a fourteen and all that junk. But he told me that he loves me. And I trust him." The corner of her mouth curved into a smile, and her eyes lit up. "I trust him and I love him."

"Then I'm happy for you," I said, my own smile not coming nearly as naturally. Because I knew what Elise didn't: the reason Chris had dumped her in the first place. And the reason why he might end up dumping her again. Or worse.

Chris was a vamp, exactly like me. Except *not* exactly like me. He didn't feed from humans anymore, but he had once. That very first kill. And now he was stuck a vampire. Unlike some of the vamps I'd met at school, though, Chris wasn't too bad. And his hatred of Stephen Wills had pretty much equaled my own.

That didn't mean he wouldn't give in to the hunger eventually, though. Unlike me, he didn't have anything to lose.

I turned away from Elise, frowning a bit. A vamp with a human girlfriend. Somehow, I didn't see it working out for Chris and Elise.

Strangely, that gave me hope. Maybe Clayton was trying to have me killed, but if we could get past *that* little issue, then at least we were both on the same footing. Either both vamps or both humans.

That was something, right?

Chapter 11

I didn't encounter any more stalkers on the way home, but I still couldn't shake the feeling that I was being watched. I moved fast and turned around often, but I never saw anyone. At least, I never saw anyone until I made it home. Then I saw a figure in the driveway across the street from my house. I stared at it, trying to decide if it was a person or simply an odd shadow.

When the light came on in the house, I had my answer. *Clayton.* Watching me, but saying nothing.

I took a step toward him, determined. *He* couldn't kill me, after all. And I wanted him to say to my face that he wasn't my boyfriend anymore. (A *duh* moment if ever there was one, but I really had to hear it.)

I made it all of two steps, and then chickened out. I'm a total and complete relationship wimp, but that wasn't the only reason I put on the brakes. I'd also realized that just because *he* couldn't kill me, that didn't mean Clayton didn't have a willing minion standing by, ready to take me out.

Yikes!

On that depressing and terrifying note, I raced inside, then slammed the door and bolted it. Just in case.

All in all, not the way to start an evening in a good mood. Quite the contrary, actually, and by the time I'd made it back into my bedroom, I was feeling altogether surly, my surliness made worse by the fact that I couldn't peek out my bedroom windows to see if he was still there, watching me.

Or, rather, I *could* peek out, but it would be a big hassle. My bedroom is bright and airy. Or it was before the big change to vampdom. After that, I'd covered my windows with foil and thick green garbage bags, all of which is a real pain to take off. So now my room is dark and musty, lit only by the umpteen billion lights and candles I keep around the place.

Which meant that instead of keeping tabs on my boyfriend, I was stuck doing nothing, without any contact whatsoever with the outside world. Sure, I had my television, cell phone, and the Internet. But other than that, I was totally isolated.

Normally, I don't mind being alone. Tonight, it felt all creepy.

So instead of kicking back and reading a book, I woke up my computer and IM'd Jenny. Too bad for me, Jenny didn't IM back.

"Darn it, Jenn!" I said to my computer. "What are you doing? Sleeping? Studying?" Weren't best friends supposed to be permanently on call?

I clicked over to my e-mail, read a thousand spam messages, and was on the verge of shutting the whole machine down, when a new message arrived. Naturally, I clicked on it, then right away wished I hadn't:

Find the formula
Or else

Oh.
Uh-oh.
And, in case that didn't fully express my feelings on the matter: *Oh. My. Gosh.*

I looked at the e-mail more closely, realized the e-mail address it came from was completely bogus, and decided to freak out a little.

I yanked up my cell phone and dialed Jenny, but she didn't answer. Where was she?

I paced my room, pondering that question. For that matter, where was I? And what was I doing?

I'd stopped looking for the formula, because I didn't have Stephen breathing down my neck anymore. And the only reason I'd been looking for it in the first place was because he'd pretty much said I'd be more dead if I didn't.

From the looks of that e-mail, I was right back in the same position. Only this time, I didn't know who to be pissed off at.

My cell phone rang and I snatched it up. "Jenny! I got a message about the—"

"It's Tamara," came the cold voice from the other end.

"Oh," I said. And then I realized I knew *exactly* who to be angry at. "Tell me about the formula," I demanded. "Who wants it? And what happens if I don't make it?"

"Um, hello? I really need you to focus here, Beth. The formula is so not the big."

"It's not?" I asked glancing at my computer. "Didn't you

call because I'd read my e-mail?" The timing was too perfect. The e-mail had to have one of those read-confirmation thingies on it.

"Um, no," she said. "I'm really not that interested in your stupid e-mail."

"Okay, wait. Earlier you were all hyped about convincing me to find the formula," I said. "What gives?"

"*Nelson* was all hyped," she said. "Me, I'm not particularly caring."

"Why not? I thought you wanted the formula, too. So that you could be daylight girl after they turned you into a vampire."

"I do," she said, but I was pretty sure I heard some hesitation there. Maybe she wasn't feeling the vampire love as much anymore? "But maybe I don't believe you're the one to find the thing. You're not Albert Einstein. You're *you*." She said it with the same tone she might use if she'd stepped in dog doo.

"So what's your point?"

"That everyone's acting like you're the second coming of the chemistry messiah or something. It's absurd."

I wanted to argue, but the truth was, I'd been thinking pretty much the same thing myself. So I sat down and spun around in my desk chair until I started to feel dizzy. "Okay," I finally said. "I give up. If it wasn't about the formula, then why'd you call?"

"Cheerleading," she said. "Why else would I talk to you?"

"That's a really good question, Tam."

"Look, I'm not exactly crying any tears over you dropping off the team, but the fact is that you're our sixth. And we can't do the pyramid at the assembly tomorrow if you're not there. So if you're going to quit, can you at least wait until after Christmas break?"

"You've got to be kidding me! I'm a freaking vampire because of you, and now you think I should do you a favor?"

"Um, hello? You almost broke my nose! I think we're even."

"We are so not even, Tamara. Not even close."

"Fine," she said, and I could totally hear her gritting her teeth. "Do this, and I'll try to convince Ladybell not to put something nasty in your permanent record when you do quit the team. There. How's that?"

"Not bad," I said. Ladybell—yes, that's really her name—coached both the drill team and the cheerleading squad. She's one of those stick-thin blonde women who wears too much blue eyeshadow, and she's *totally* into the whole drill team thing. Too much into it, if you know what I mean. Me quitting would likely be taken as a slap in her face, resulting in lots of nasty red words on my permanent record. Which meant that Tamara's offer did have a certain appeal. I'd get the benefit of being a cheerleader, and I wouldn't have to stick it out for both semesters. "You swear?"

"Yes, yes, I swear."

I closed my eyes. "Okay. I'll do it."

"Yeah? Fabulous. Okay, so get to assembly at least twenty minutes early, and for God's sake, make sure your uniform is clean, okay?"

"I'll be there when I'm there, Tamara. Now say thank you, and hang up."

I grinned at the phone, waiting for her to comply. Because at the moment, I was holding all the cards, and I knew it. Not terribly exciting cards, but important to Tamara, and that felt really, really good.

"Thank you," she said. And then I heard that satisfying click.

I took another celebratory spin in my desk chair, stopping only when another thought hit me. *Holding all the cards.* Maybe that's what the formula was—my full house. If

I actually managed to work out the formula—if I could control the power to walk during the day—then I'd be the one with the bargaining power. And like Mr. Tucker said, I'd have the pride and fulfillment of a job well done.

Always listen to your teachers, right?

Chapter 12

"**W**e've got spirit! Yes, we do! We've got spirit! How 'bout you?"

Me and Tamara and Stacy and the rest of the cheerleaders were screaming at the top of our lungs. And, yes, I really was screaming, totally getting into the whole school spirit thing. I had to. I didn't want to give Tamara any ammunition for backing out on our deal.

The assembly was to introduce the members of the basketball team, newly auditioned and now decked out in their basketball uniforms. Some local celebrity who used to play basketball for Waterloo was there, too, and we were all waiting with wild anticipation (not) for his speech.

Considering I didn't care about basketball or local politics,

I wasn't overwhelmingly thrilled about the fact that we were missing all of first and second periods. Two hours seemed a bit much.

About that, I was absolutely right. We did our cheerleader thing right off the bat, and then we got stuck in tiny metal chairs. Uncomfortable tiny metal chairs. From that vantage point I had nothing to do except look at the crowd.

So that's what I did.

I looked at each face, one by one, wondering who'd orchestrated turning me into a vampire. Unfortunately for me, no one had a big, red V stamped on their forehead, which meant I was as clueless at the end of the assembly as I'd been at the beginning.

"About the only thing interesting," I told Jenny as we were *finally* leaving the gym, "was that Clayton watched me the whole time."

"In a good way? Or a bad way?"

I looked at her sideways. "I don't know. I chickened out when I tried to talk to him."

Her shoulders slumped, her pain at my patheticness clear. "God, Beth. Just open your mouth and *talk*. You're good at that."

"No," I said, shaking my head. "*You're* good at that. I suck at boyfriends. Remember Larry Stein?"

"The guy you went steady with in eighth grade? Yeah. So?"

"So I'm technically still going steady," I said. "We never broke up." Her eyebrows lifted at that, but I barreled on. "I was too chicken to tell him I didn't even like him that much, which is why we started going steady in the first place. And then I was too chicken to break up."

She blinked at me. "So what happened?"

"Different high schools," I said. "I played the avoidance card. He went away. Problem solved."

"You really are pathetic," she said, her voice filled with wonder.

Sad, but true, I thought. The truth was that I really did need to talk to Clayton. And if I hadn't been functionally brain-dead from sitting through two hours of assembly, maybe I could have worked up the nerve.

I commented on my own pitifulness with a low growling noise of self-disgust, which made Jenny look sideways at me and then raise her eyebrows. "Don't growl. It makes you sound all vampy."

That made me laugh. "Where were you last night, anyway? I tried to call you." I tugged her off to the side, and then filled her in on how Nelson and Tamara had cornered me, and then about how later on I'd gotten the e-mail about finding the formula. And about Tamara's deal.

"I was wondering what you were doing," she said, indicating my uniform. "I didn't want to ask. In case you were having a psychotic moment or something."

"Careful," I said, "or I'll growl again."

"But seriously," she said, "it sounds like Nelson's stepped up to take Stephen's place."

"Right," I said. "The big, bad vampire leader needs another flunkie." I frowned, thinking that over. "You know what? It really does make sense that my maker sent Stephen to do his dirty work. He *wanted* me to believe that Stephen was my master. That way he learned whether or not I had the cojones to take him out."

"And you *so* totally did." We look at each other, and Jenny makes a face. "Oh. Maybe that's not so good after all. Now he's going to lay low and be even harder to find."

"But not impossible," I said. "Tamara and Nelson must be working for him. And if they're working for him, then they must know who he is. And if that's the case, then I can make them talk."

"Maybe," she said.

"What do you mean maybe?" I asked, deflating a bit. "I can be persuasive."

"Well, I guess I mean that Tamara may not actually know. What with her not yet being a vamp and all. And Nelson may have some hoochey on him so that if he tells you he turns into smoke or something."

"Hoochey?" I repeat.

"Black magic," she says, looking at me with serious eyes. "Like all that stuff that Clayton's grandfather was talking about."

"I know what you meant," I said. "But I repeat: *hoochey?*"

"Shut up," she said.

I did. I really didn't have a choice. I was laughing too hard to say anything at all.

"You're lucky I'm even helping you, you know."

"I know," I said, nodding seriously. "It's dangerous and I really appreciate it. You could get slammed with some hoochey or something."

She smacked me with her purse, but I could see the smile under the anger.

"So how do we avoid the hoochey?" I asked. "If Nelson can't actually tell me who the master is, how will we find out?"

"I guess we'll have to follow them around and do the James Bond thing. I'll bring the trenchcoat."

"I'll bring the dark sunglasses," I said. "It completes the chic look for today's vampire female."

"Convenient," she said, "since you look really good in black."

"And I—" I didn't finish the thought, though, because I'd caught a look at her face. "What?"

"I was thinking," she said, stopping to lean against a "Just Say No" poster. "The e-mail threatened you, right? So maybe *they're* the ones trying to kill you. Maybe it's not Clayton at all."

For a split second, my whole body felt lighter. "You think?" But before she could answer, I crashed back down to earth again. "No, that doesn't make sense. For one, why was he watching me? And for another, they're threatening me if I *don't* make the formula. Why would they kill me before giving me a chance?"

"Oh. Right. Good point. I guess I wanted someone to be out to kill you other than Clayton."

"Thanks so much."

"You know what I mean."

"Yeah," I said. "I do."

"Speaking of romance," Jenny said, "did you see Mr. Tucker?"

I rolled my eyes, because the idea of thousand-year-old Mr. Tucker and romance was totally icky. "They were *not* flirting," I said, trying to erase from my brain what I'd seen with my own two eyes: Mr. Tucker and Ladybell standing *way* too close to each other.

"They were *totally* flirting," Jenny argued. "Didn't you see the way he was leaning toward her? He obviously thinks she's hot."

"Ick!" I put my hands over my ears, wondering how on earth I'd look at Mr. Tucker during tomorrow's Latin class. "Not listening, not listening!"

"At least someone's got a little boyfriend action going," Jenny said morbidly. "I don't even have a date to the dance, and your boyfriend is trying to kill you."

"Thanks," I said. "Thanks so much for the reminder."

Chapter 13

There are certain advantages to being universally acknowledged as the smartest girl in school. Class skippage being way up there in the perks department.

Which was how I came to skip world history and spend that hour in Mr. Jordan's empty chemistry lab. "Thanks for letting me use your off period to work on my science fair project," I said. A huge lie, but the gratitude was genuine.

"Anything to help," he said. He pointed to his wall, along which were several years of science awards. "I need another blue ribbon on my board."

I said something noncommittal, then sort of fiddled around until he—finally!—went back into the office area and I had the room for myself. Then I continued to fiddle around in front of a Bunsen burner, hoping inspiration would strike. The fact was, I had no idea what I was doing. I'd spent way too much time looking at my blood under a microscope and seeing . . . *nothing*. I'd read all sorts of stuff about vitamin D and UV lights and general vampire lore. And still, I'd managed to figure out nothing. I was using the resources of my part-time hospital job to poke around and investigate the whole vamp-formula mystery.

Still, no luck.

Not exactly great for a girl's ego, you know?

The fact is, I couldn't shake what Tamara had said. I'm smart, but I'm only in high school. It's not like my cup runneth over with scientific know-how.

That's actually one of the things that has really been bugging me about this whole daywalking formula thing. The vamps had some ancient Latin text they needed translated, and then they needed somebody with the scientific hoo-ha to understand the riddle and make the formula set out in the text. Okay, fine. But why me?

I'm smart and all, but let's get real. Vampires couldn't find someone a teensy bit more qualified? The whole situation was completely bizarre.

And it's not like their stupid Latin text made any sense. Why is it that ancient documents with dark secrets always have to be so vague? Take this one for example:

> Draw close, dark apprentice, and learn the truth. The path out of the darkness and into the freedom of the sun has been forged. The secret rests with the first of us, whose blood intoxicates as wine, yet holds the truth for he who would reveal it. Ancestor and heir, self and same.
>
> We crave the secret and seek the knowledge. Locate the talisman and gather the light. To you, dark apprentice, I assign these tasks. Lift the night, and free us all.

Clear as mud, huh? And yet I'm supposed to figure out not only what it means but also how to make the formula. Because everyone in the vamp community seems to agree that the text refers to a formula to let vampires walk during the day. And since I'm pretty convinced that the blood reference means that vampire blood is key, that's what I've been focusing on.

What I *don't* have is the talisman that the riddle talks about. And I have a feeling that without that doohickey, I'm not going to get very far. But I have to try. First Stephen and now my new e-mail buddy. They'd pretty much convinced me. Don't try, and I'd be dead before I had the chance to un-undead myself.

I already had the threat of girlfriend-icide hanging over my head. I really didn't need to be double-tagged by a surly vampire master, pissed off that I wasn't searching for his magic potion.

So there I was, looking. Looking, but not finding, because I'd already tried pretty much everything. Honestly, the situation entirely sucked.

I was sitting there thinking about the overall suckiness of my life when Chris Freytag sauntered in. "How goes it?"

I made a face.

"That good, huh?"

"Why are you here?" Chris and I had ended up on a friendly note, but that had come only after he'd tricked me. And almost got himself fried by the daylight because of it. I'd thought, though, that we were back on track. Hearing about how he was back with Elise—and hadn't told her about the whole vamp situation—made me a little nervous.

"I came to help you," he said.

"What about Elise?" I asked, my hands on my hips and my mind *so* not on whatever help he had to offer.

His forehead crinkled. "What about her?"

"You haven't told her, Chris. She has a right to know."

He looked down at the ground. "I know. I'm afraid that if I tell her, she'll dump me again."

"If she finds out on her own, she'll dump you that much faster."

"Look, I know. But this isn't about Elise." He frowned. "Or maybe it is. Nelson's gone all freaky."

"Nelson was already freaky," I said.

"True enough, but now he's convinced that he's supposed to have this daywalking formula. And that if you don't make it, he needs to get rid of you so that the master will find someone else to do it."

I perked up. "He knows who the master is? Do you know?"

"I don't have a clue," Chris said. "I always thought it was Stephen, same as you. But Nelson . . ." He trailed off with a shrug. "Maybe he does know who the master is. He sure seems to be taking orders from someone."

I squinted at him over my Bunsen burner. "What do you mean?"

"You haven't noticed?"

I cocked my head. "Noticed what?"

"He's been making more vamps," he said. "Only *he's* not making them. He's making them the same way we were made."

I swallowed. "With the master's blood?"

"Exactly."

"Why?" I asked. "And who?"

He rolled his eyes. "Girls mostly. He takes them out under the bleachers, makes them a drink, kisses them a little, and then—"

"Yeah," I said in a whisper. "I know the drill." I knew it all too well. A full vampire—like Nelson or Chris or Stephen—had the power to use a "glamour"—basically a spell. They could more or less hypnotize. Which made it easy to get a girl to drink, oh, say, a Bloody Mary under the bleachers. And if the "bloody" wasn't tomato juice but actual blood, well, then Nelson could be creating a whole crew of girl vamps.

Wasn't that great?

"How many?" I asked. "How many has he made?"

"Only two or three," he said. "But I think he'll make more." He looked up at me, his eyes full of fear. "And I'm afraid he'll do it to Elise."

Chapter 14

My convo with Chris kept me on edge for the rest of the day, and I kept looking at the faces of girls in the hall, wondering if they'd been turned.

I wasn't worried about the cheerleaders. They were down with the whole vampire thing, and from what I could tell, they'd been promised eternal un-death once the daywalking formula was found. Can't have a cheerleader who can't go out in the sun, after all.

But Elise? Frumpy Elise who barely showed her face, inside or outside school? Yeah, I could see why Chris was worried.

I met Jenny in the journalism room after school and filled her in.

"Whoa," she said. "Do you know who's been turned?"

I shook my head. "I've been watching faces, but none of the girls look vampy. Maybe they're staying away from the school?"

"Maybe," she said. "And maybe we need to do something to keep him from turning anyone else?"

"No kidding. But what?"

"Kill Nelson?" she suggested.

I considered the idea and decided it had a lot of merit. I couldn't do it, of course, what with the whole same-branch-of-the-vamp-family-tree thing. And I didn't want Jenny to do it, since she could end up dead—or worse. But maybe Kevin . . . ?

"You can ask," Jenny said when I suggested the idea. "I bet he'd be up for it. So long as you remember to ask," she added. "And don't get distracted by smooches."

I narrowed my eyes. "Jealous much?"

"Not even. You may have a college guy kissing you, but I *so* don't want your problems."

"No kidding," I said, then sighed. "So I'll ask Kevin to take care of Nelson. But what do we do in the meantime? About the girls, I mean?"

Jenny smiled. "Leave that to me."

Since I was more than happy to dump a responsibility on

someone else, I agreed. Then I nodded at her desk and the pile of photographs spread out on the battered wood. A laptop was open in front of her, and when I gestured to it, she broke into a wide grin.

She was about to tell me what she'd found when the door opened and Randy, the sports editor, walked in. "Yo, girls," he said, then tossed his backpack on a desk and pulled out an algebra book, huddling down for the count. Not unusual—we all used the room to do homework—but I really wanted him gone.

So did Jenny. Obviously she'd found something. But unless I wanted Randy to hear all about my vampiric trials and tribulations, we were going to have to wait until we could wrangle a private conversation.

"How's the column coming?" I asked, since I really couldn't keep my mouth shut.

"Oh, great," she said, and I could tell from her expression that she was talking about Operation Daylight Exposure. *Not* whatever real column she happened to be planning for the week.

"Jenny's punting," Randy said, abandoning algebra. "She's been pouring over those pictures all day. Some pansy-ass column idea. So much for hard-hitting investigative journalism."

Randy and Jenny have been feuding ever since she told him that sports reporting was nothing more than announcing the scores for a bunch of mindless, gladiating, testosterone junkies. Randy really hadn't taken that well.

Now, Jenny shot him a nasty look. "There's nothing wrong with doing a lighter column every once in a while. Is there, Beth?"

But I wasn't answering. Instead, I was watching the door.

Jenny turned to see where I was staring. "Oh," she said as Clayton walked in. "Hi."

He completely ignored her, looking only at me. "Hey, Beth," he said. "I think we need to talk."

Chapter 15

Since we couldn't talk in front of Randy, Clayton and I went into Ms. Shelby's office. Technically off-limits, but these were extenuating circumstances.

I settled myself behind Ms. Shelby's desk and waited for him to talk. Hopefully, the fact that the office had glass windows that looked out over the classroom meant that he wasn't there to somehow kill me. Homicide in front of witnesses is really bad karma.

Actually, though, I wasn't too worried. I'd made Clayton, which meant that he couldn't kill me directly. I—being above him on that undead family tree—wasn't suffering from the same disability. In other words, I was safe. For the moment, anyway.

Just in case, though, I stayed behind the desk. And I kept a pencil in my hand. A wooden number two pencil. Stupid, maybe. But it made me feel better.

"I saw you in the caf," I said, since the conversation was definitely dragging. "And at the assembly. How come you didn't come over and talk to me?"

Man, I sounded so normal. Amazing in and of itself, but it totally begged the question of why I wasn't throwing things at him and demanding that he explain himself. Honestly, this teenage relationship stuff is hard.

Clayton looked at me sideways. "Me? You're the one avoiding me."

"I am not!" I crossed my arms over my chest and took a step backward. "Okay, maybe I am a little, but I have to say I have a darn good reason." I lifted my chin. "Wouldn't you say?"

"*You* have a reason? Come on, Beth! You're the one who—"

"Who what?"

"Oh, come on! You *kissed* him. I stood there and watched while you kissed *Kevin*."

"I . . . oh. Well . . ." I shifted uneasily in the chair. I'd been prepared for a battle about the up- and downsides of killing me. I'd even been prepared to tell him I understood why he'd do it, although I wasn't willing to go so far as to actually condone it.

But this? This was way unfamiliar territory. Suddenly I was the one facing accusations, and I wasn't too sure I liked it.

I raised my chin. "You were spying on me? Isn't that a little bit low?"

"Not any lower than kissing another guy," he said, his voice rising with his temper. "And I wasn't spying. You told me where you'd be."

"How lucky for you. You knew exactly where to send your friend with the crossbow."

He flinched. "Ex*cuse* me?"

"Convenient, wasn't it? Me telling you exactly where I was? Makes the whole assassinate-your-girlfriend thing *so* much easier."

"Did you spike your blood with bad Vivarin or something? Because you are totally tripping."

I shook my head, the pressure in my eyes almost unbearable. My body wanted to cry, but I couldn't. And that only made me madder. "Don't play games with me, Clayton. After everything we've been through I think I deserve better than that."

Since he was still silent, I took a menacing step toward

him. "You. Tried. To. Have. Me. Killed." I clenched my hands into fists. It felt oddly liberating saying it out loud like that.

His eyes narrowed until they were nothing more than black slits. "What gave you that idea?"

"Oh, I don't know. Maybe the phone conversation I overheard at the trailer? You know. The one where you were talking details with the guy who'd barely missed my heart with his arrow."

All the color drained from his face. "Beth," he said, taking a step toward me.

I held a hand out to keep him at bay. "Don't even," I said. "And don't you dare come a step closer."

I looked out the window toward the journalism room. So far, Randy hadn't noticed that we were only seconds away from going at each other's throats. Jenny could tell, though. And from her expression, she wasn't sure if she should sit still or go pull the fire alarm and evac the school. At the very least, that would be a distraction.

"So you heard my conversation," Clayton said. He leaned against the wall and crossed his arms over his chest, his eyes bearing down on me, his face totally serious. He was wearing his army-green flak jacket, which only added to the macho soldier-of-fortune look. At the moment I was more than willing to believe he'd kill me on the spot if he could. I also wanted nothing more than to have him hold me tight and tell me that all of this was a bad dream. That everything was okay between us, and that I'd get my life back.

I steeled myself, though, forcing down boyfriend-lust thoughts in favor of survival.

I lifted my chin. "Your grandpa let me in, and I . . ." I trailed off with a shrug. "I heard what you were trying to do, and so I left."

"And you immediately thought I was trying to kill you?"

"I'm not an idiot, Clayton," I said. "My GPA's higher than yours. So don't even think about denying it."

"Yeah, you're smart all right." He looked at me for a long time, then shook his head. "I won't deny it. And you won't have to worry about avoiding me anymore. We're through, Beth. I'm outta here."

Chapter 16

"He *admitted* it?"

"Well, he didn't deny it," I said, feeling surly. All things considered, I thought Clayton was too busy being pissed off at me to engage in any active denial. "But I think the bigger issue here is that he broke up with me. *He* broke up with *me*! After what he did!"

"He's scum," she said, in loyal-best-friend fashion.

We were in Jenny's car, and she was looking at me instead of at the road.

"Um, Jenny? I think that's a red light."

She slammed on the brakes, skidding to a stop about two centimeters from the bumper of a brand-new Mercedes. She didn't even blink. She turned to me and repeated, "But did he not deny it in a he-did-it way? Or in a he's-pissed-at-you-for-thinking-he-did-it way?"

"I really don't want to talk about it." I'd been thinking about it for the last hour, trying to get my head around the situation. Had he broken up with me because I'd wrongly accused him of trying to kill me? Or because I'd found him out? His indignation had sure seemed genuine—and I *so* didn't want to believe that my boyfriend had tried to kill me—but at the same time, he wasn't my boyfriend anymore.

So much for sticking together through the rough patches, huh?

"That scum," Jenny said. "That scum-sucking, slime-mongering, weenie-faced *scum*."

"Weenie-faced?"

She waved a hand. "It popped into my head. It sounds pathetic, and that's exactly what he is. Pathetic."

"I guess . . ."

She looked at me askance. "Do *not* tell me that you're sympathizing with him. You're my best friend. He absolutely, totally, one hundred percent is not allowed to kill you."

"I kinda think maybe he didn't." Which, of course, opened the door to a whole new question—who did? But I wasn't going there yet.

"Even so," Jenny said, still on a roll. "He's also not allowed to break up with you. Those are the rules, and he's just going to have to deal."

"Thanks." The light changed and she tapped the accelerator, inching forward as I let my head fall back against the headrest. I'm not sure why I was in such a funk. I guess I'd been living under the fantasy that the second I saw Clayton, he'd pull me into his arms, kiss me, and explain how it had all been a big misunderstanding. Instead, he dumped me.

Talk about shifting a girl's perspective!

"You doing okay?" she asked, downshifting from irate to sympathetic.

"I guess. Not what I expected, you know? I mean, he was my *boyfriend*. We're supposed to be gossiping about whether or not I let him get to second base. Not speculating on whether he tried to have me killed. And we haven't even been going out long enough to break up. I mean, we're hardly out of the grace period."

"At least you're handling it well," she said with a smile, to which I responded with an eyebrow raise, since my whininess so far had not telegraphed well adjusted. "You're making jokes," she clarified. "That's good, right?"

"If you say so." We drove a few blocks in silence—what

was there to say after that?—until I decided I was being annoying and morbid. Yes, the slime-mongering creep may—possibly, maybe, I couldn't completely rule it out—have tried to kill me. And yes, the scum-sucking loser broke up with me. But was I going to let that spoil all my fun? No way. I wasn't about to give him the satisfaction. "Find anything in the photo archives?"

"Changing the subject much?"

I was, but I denied it anyway. "It's all the same subject to me. Vamps, vamps, and more vamps."

"You said it."

Something about her tone made me turn sideways in my seat to look at her. "What do you mean?"

"While you and Clayton were in the office not killing each other, I did some more work on Operation Daylight Exposure. Derek, Ennis, Nelson, and Stephen. Those were the ones I started with. Kind of like a control group, you know?"

Derek and Ennis were dead—Ennis by a vampire hunter who hung in Kevin's circle, and Derek because of Clayton—who happened to be saving me at the time.

"No outside pictures, right?" I asked.

She grinned, displaying the perfect teeth that her former Miss Texas mother had paid a fortune for. "None except football pics. And they were completely covered in uniforms and greasepaint."

That had been a big mystery for us for a while—how the guys had played football while they were vamps—but we'd finally figured it out. Instead of doing the black gunk under their eye routine, they blacked out their entire faces. And they wore gloves. If these guys weren't so guy-like, it would have seemed girlie. Or at the very least, bizarre. As it was, they'd practically started a fashion statement for the macho jock.

The cheerleaders, though, couldn't follow suit. No one wants to see a cute girl in a tiny uniform covered in greasy black goo. So although the girls sucked vamp blood to make them stronger, they were waiting for the daywalking formula before they were changed to vamps.

Frankly, I thought they were nuts. From my conversation with Tamara, she might be beginning to think so, too.

"It's hard to decide if someone has no outdoor pics because they're a vamp, or because they weren't outside when the photographer was. But I do think I clued in to at least a few possible suspects."

"Yeah? How?"

"Group pictures," she said, then smiled. "Am I good, or what?"

"You're good," I said. Group pictures at Waterloo are taken at the school in front of a huge granite statute of the State of Texas. Bleachers are permanently set up during picture week, and if it rains, the shoot is rescheduled. The school paid too much for that stupid statue for it not to make multiple appearances in every single yearbook.

"So you made lists of who wasn't in the group pics?"

"Exactly. Since we've got the list of all the various club and class members, it was easy. Time-consuming, but easy. And then I cross-referenced all the groups, so that I could eliminate someone who might have been absent on picture day."

"You're like Nancy Drew," I said.

"Great," she said. "I'm a holdover from antiquity."

"Better than being Miss Marple," I said. "At least Nancy had a cool car."

She rolled her eyes. "Do you want to hear the details or not?"

"Yes, please."

"Most of our vamp suspects are from the popular kids group. The kind who'd want their picture in the yearbook group photos, you know?"

"The kind that wouldn't have skipped the group picture unless they didn't have a choice."

"Exactly."

"You said they were *mostly* popular kids. What about the others?"

"That's what's freaky. The rest are the total opposite of popular. Kids like Tiko and Marlene."

Tiko and Marlene have been dating since about first grade, which was about the time they started smoking and drinking. To say they were the opposite of popular was pretty much the understatement of the year. "They might have decided to blow off group pictures," I said.

"Maybe. But if you were in the market to make a vampire—"

"—why not go with the black-fingernail-polish, practically-already-a-vamp crowd? Yeah. I see your point."

"It's only a guess," she said. "But it makes sense. And if we already know that Nelson is out there still making vampires . . ."

"Then it's starting to look like he's making even more than Chris thought. Plus he's being smart about it. The Tikos and the popular kids can skip classes without anyone blinking. So if they're dodging sunlight, no one's going to notice. Not right away, anyway. If I can figure out how to go to school without frying, they can, too."

"A sad commentary on the public school system," Jenny said, with a grave nod of her head.

"It might not all be Nelson," I said. "Maybe Stephen lied." I'd asked Stephen if they'd been turning a lot of the kids at school into vampires, and he'd pretty much told me no. Later I'd found out that they were being selective, waiting to increase the vampire population once I'd given them the daywalking formula. Gee, it was nice to feel needed.

"Maybe he lied," Jenny said. "Or maybe he didn't know."

That was a good point, and I looked at her with respect. "And you think you're not going to ace your SATs," I said. "Jenny, you're brilliant."

"Brilliant, but unappreciated. Do you think that's it?"

"Stephen was a pawn," I said, "the same as me. And now Nelson's a pawn."

"Which we already know," Jenny said. "So much for my brilliance."

"It makes it more clear that we have to find my maker. Once we do that, we can cure me. And we can shut down the Waterloo High vampire factory."

"Maybe the maker is actually a student," Jenny said. "Stephen was hundreds of years old, remember?"

I nodded, because I'd thought of that. "Yeah, except that Stephen was a transfer student. Most of these kids we've known since preschool. It's the teachers who change all the time."

"That's true," she said. "I'm still sorting through the faculty and staff photos. We'll see who pops up."

Behind us, someone honked his horn. We were in the little circular drive in front of the hospital, and since you're not supposed to park there, I opened my door and stuck one foot outside. "This was really great work," I said, meaning it. The news about the growing vamp population was interesting, even if I didn't have a clue what to do with it.

"Wait," she called, before I could slam the door. "What are you going to do about Clayton?"

"I don't know," I said. For a few minutes, I'd been so absorbed in broader vamp issues that I'd forgotten that little personal problem of the killer boyfriend. "Mostly I guess I'll watch my back."

"I'll watch it, too," she said. "As much as I can, anyway."

The car behind us honked again, and I slammed the door. Jenny drove off, and I figured that meant that her role as back-watcher for the day was done. I was alone at the hospital and on my own.

Hopefully, I wouldn't die on the night shift.

Chapter 17

I survived that night shift, and the next one as well, so when I got to the lab on Sunday, I was feeling pretty confident that I'd make it through that night too without being assassinated.

"So what's new with your science fair project?" Cary asked me after I'd settled in at my work area. He's the head tech, and has been my boss ever since my dad got me a part-time job in the hospital lab.

"Slower than I'd hoped," I said, feeling a little guilty that I'd spent most of the weekend on my own personal business instead of my job stuff.

Cary grunted, then turned his attention to a beeping centrifuge. Just as well, since I didn't want to be grilled on the details of my nonexistent project. An inconvenient truth, since I'd been using the lab to work on this phantom project for quite a while now.

My dad and Cary had even been helping me, passing me liters of blood for my personal use, all in the interest of science, of course. In fact about the only thing Cary wouldn't do for me was run a DNA test. I'd begged him to put my blood through the ringer, but he'd firmly declined, citing all sorts of mumbo jumbo about hospital property and overwhelming expense.

Well, sure. But I *needed* that test!

He'd been adamant, though, and so I'd finally quit bugging him about it. Instead, I'd done everything I could up to DNA testing. But so far the fruits of my overwhelming productivity were precisely nada.

I came to the lab today, though, with a new plan. Or at least the bones of a new plan. I'd been thinking about it for most of the afternoon, ever since I'd reread the formula riddle and decided it was a crock of idiocy.

Vamp blood had to be the key; that much seemed clear enough. But the trouble was that I didn't know enough about my new blood on a genetic/molecular level.

What I needed was to do a comparison—match my new blood against my old blood. A perfect plan, really, with only one tiny problem. I'd never donated any of my prevamp blood. So what was I supposed to compare it with?

I was pondering that problem when Cary finished up with the centrifuge. "Sorry about that," he said. "Delicate business, and I didn't want to get distracted. But you've got my full attention now." As if to illustrate the point, he sat down, propped his chin on his fist, and nodded. "Shoot."

"Uh," I said, because what was I *supposed* to say?

He held up a hand. "Before you ask, though, I've got to tell you that I'm going to have a problem getting any more blood."

"Oh." Pangs of hunger poked at my stomach. I'd been more than happy to resort to a bit of stealing before, but lately, I hadn't been able to get anywhere close to the blood. Daddy and Cary were my lifeline. Literally. "Um, why?"

"Blood's been locked up tight. An edict from the administrative level. Apparently, we've got a shortage."

I nodded, hoping I didn't look like a major cause of that shortage. "Don't worry," I said. "I'll survive." On rats. Yuck.

"You're a terrible liar," he said. He sighed. "Look, kid, I'm sorry. I remember when I was trying to pull together my project for the state science fair. I went through samples and specimens like toilet paper."

I cringed a little at the metaphor, but nodded.

"So don't think I don't know where you're coming from. Sure you've been using a lot of blood, but sometimes you have to kill a few pint bags in the quest for knowledge, right?"

"Absolutely," I said, my mouth practically watering at the thought of a pint bag. Or four.

"So how can I help?"

"You mean other than getting me the blood?"

"Can't do that anymore, but I figure you must be right smack in the middle of your project. Big blow. Just about breaks my heart. Want to make it up to you."

He was pacing now, checking dials and levels, his words coming staccato as he efficiently marched through the lab.

"I could sure use that DNA analysis," I said, absolutely certain he'd say no again. But what did I have to lose?

He stopped, his hand on the control button for some new machine with a lot of flashing lights. He stared at me for a minute, and then he nodded. "I shouldn't. Administration audits the use of that machine, and it could mean my ass. But . . ."

He trailed off, probably waiting for me to jump in and stop him from offering to put his rear end on the line. I wasn't about to do that, though. The old Beth would have. The old Beth was nice and sweet and terribly worried about whether or not other people got in trouble on her behalf.

But the new Beth?

New Beth figured people could take care of themselves. More important, New Beth really wanted that DNA analysis.

"Right," Cary said. "I think I can manage it under the table for you. An analysis of your blood, right?"

I was about to nod when a remarkable thing happened: my dad walked in, and I conceived a brilliant plan. I needed a comparison. And if I didn't have any of my own prevamp blood stashed away, then a blood relative was the next best thing.

I held up a finger to Cary and went over to my father. "Daddy," I said, taking his arm and leading him to the phlebotomist chair in the corner of the lab. "I need a little favor. Actually, I need a little blood."

Daddy didn't protest, which was both good and expected. After all, I didn't get the car he'd semi-promised for my birthday, so I knew he was suffering under the weight of parental guilt, made all the more keen by the fact that he and my mom had recently divorced, leaving me as yet another teenage statistic.

And as far as pushing my science project, Daddy was as hyped as Cary was about me advancing to State. Not like there's pressure on me or anything . . .

I turned back to Cary, smiling broadly. "Not an analysis," I said, pointing to Daddy. "A comparison."

I might not completely understand the results when I got them back, but at least I'd have a sample of unvamped family blood to compare to my newly vamped DNA. It might not help, but it couldn't hurt.

Although considering the size of the syringe Cary was now wielding, I realized that it might sting a little . . .

Chapter 18

I worked from six-thirty to after midnight, and by the time I left the lab, my stomach was a tight little knot of hunger, and I was in a particularly cranky mood. Trust me: PMS has nothing on a hungry vampire.

Daddy drove me home, though, so I had to keep my crankiness in check. After all, he'd bled for me. (And can I say that it was *hard* not sinking my teeth into him while Cary was drawing blood? The aroma of blood is *way* heady, and I think I showed remarkable restraint!)

It's actually an easy bus ride from the hospital to our block, but since I've been working nights, Daddy has taken to driving me. He's technically on shift at the hospital, but the drive is short and he takes his beeper. Normally, I kind of like the few minutes of father-daughter time. Normally, though, I've fed.

"You're quiet," he said.

"Just hungry," I answered, then mentally kicked myself.

"We can drive through somewhere. Get a burger?"

"No!" I said, way too quickly.

He glanced sideways at me. "We can do Taco Bell if you'd rather."

"I'm . . . on a diet," I said. "Cheerleading."

"I thought you were going to quit cheerleading."

I turned to him. "How'd you know that?" Usually, my dad is clueless about all matters related to school. Unless, of course, the matter involves biology or chemistry or math. In which case, I'm pretty sure he's in constant e-mail contact with my teachers.

"You told your mother," he said. "Your mother told me."

"Oh." I thought about that. I *had* told my mother, but only because she'd actually been in the kitchen the day I'd come home after the whole turning-Clayton-into-a-vamp incident. I'd been so freaked—both by what happened and by seeing my workaholic mother at home—that I'd almost told her everything. I'd caught myself and managed to hit only the shareable high points. Like the fact that I'd had it with cheerleading and would be resigning from the squad posthaste.

Mom wasn't thrilled that I was planning to quit—she's big on the Pump Up Your Transcript plan—but I couldn't imagine that she'd been annoyed enough to actually call Daddy to complain. She'd opened a $500 bottle of champagne the day he'd moved out. The thought that they were actually communicating—even about me—was a little hard to fathom.

Still, I believed my dad. Unlike me, he wasn't the type to lie. If he said that Mom had told him, then told him she had. (Although maybe she told him through Marcy, her secretary?) The big question was why. And I have to say, although vampires and assassins are scary, scary things, they didn't scare me nearly as much as the idea that something must be going on with my parents. Something big. Something *huge*.

Because only something humongorific could get these two people talking.

And something humongorific sounded like more than I could handle at the moment. I already had more pressure in my life than a sixteen-year-old is supposed to have.

"Beth?" We were stopped at a red light, and my dad was staring at me. "What's the verdict?"

"Must be bad," I said, then caught myself. "Oh! I mean, it's too bad. That Mom told you I quit. I was just in a mood that day. I'm still on the squad. And that means I can't be eating burgers and fries. You know?"

"Mmmm," he said, sounding far more parental than usual. "So no dinner."

"It's the middle of the night, Dad. I'll grab some cereal at home and then crash. I'm beat."

That seemed to satisfy him, and we went the rest of the way in silence, him probably thinking about bowels and entrails and the disease of the week, and me wondering how much longer I could keep my vampiness a secret from my parents. Considering their overall cluelessness, I'd originally thought that forever was a pretty good guesstimate. Lately, though, they seemed to be paying more attention.

Lucky me.

All the more reason to ramp up my efforts to find my maker and get human again.

Daddy pulled to a stop in front of the house, then leaned over and kissed my cheek. "Get some rest," he said. I said something noncommittal and stood there as he burned rubber getting off the block. In case Mom was home, I guessed.

I slogged down our driveway to the back door. The lock on the front door tends to stick, so we hardly ever use it, coming in through the kitchen instead. I was stepping up onto the back patio when I heard the crunch of footsteps behind me. I whipped around, realizing too late that anybody interested in killing me would simply lie in wait near my house.

Idiot, idiot, idiot!

At the same time, what was I supposed to do? I was sixteen. It wasn't like I could chuck it all and check into a hotel.

Since I didn't see anyone in my yard, I started to feel a bit better. Maybe I'd heard a dog. Or a rat. After all, although an assassin *could* find me at my house, the smart assassin would do his dirty work elsewhere. Less chance of encountering my mom.

I turned back to the door, my keys in my hand, feeling a little better in a perverted sort of way. Half a second later, I was knocked to the ground, and I realized that I wasn't dealing with a smart assassin at all. For that matter, I was feeling a little stupid myself.

"You seek an abomination!" my attacker screamed, a wooden stake tight in his hand. "It must not come to pass!"

He was pale and pasty—definitely not the same guy

who'd attacked me under the Christmas lights—and even as the stake in his hand came slamming down toward my heart, I couldn't help thinking that he seemed a little bit dead for a vampire hunter. Too much time with his victims, maybe?

The thought flashed in my head and then evaporated, shoved aside by the terrifying realization that this was really happening. The crossbow's arrow may have missed my heart, but my attacker had apparently decided not to take any chances on this go-round. He was *right there*, and his aim was true.

I flinched and screamed and tried to roll to the side. Not too successfully, though. His knees were tight against my hips, and it was clear that I wasn't going anywhere.

My arms were free, though, since he was using both of his hands to hold the stake, and I balled my hand into a fist and smacked him hard in the nose. He wailed, and I got a face full of *way* putrid breath.

"You gotta get a life, dude," I said. "Vampire hunters are supposed to be cool, not grotesque," I added, managing another face punch. "Or don't you watch movies?"

"You will die," he said, and down came an arm, tight around my throat.

I immediately reached for his hand, determined to pry it

away. It was an instinctive, *stupid*, reaction, because so what if he strangled me? I was dead already, and it wasn't as if I needed to breathe.

He'd planned it, of course, and now the hand holding the stake slammed down. I had a split second to contemplate death after undeath, and then—

Nothing.

Chapter 19

*A*bsolutely *nothing*.

And I don't mean "nothing" in the philosophical sense of the word. No Nietzschean nothingness here. I mean that nothing happened.

Let me repeat that, lest you think I died (again): *Nothing. Happened.*

Or, rather, nothing happened to me. To my new buddy the vampire hunter, something big happened. He was yanked off me by someone I couldn't see from my prone position on the grass.

Immediately I was on my feet, rage having made my hunger grow. This hunter had tried to kill me, and right then

I wanted nothing more than to sink my teeth in him and call him dinner.

I lunged forward, teeth bared. I never got there, though. I heard him say "Urgh," and then I saw the pointy end of a stick emerge from his chest, plunged into his heart from the back by someone with a lot more upper-body strength than I have.

In the same instant that I realized my hunter was a vampire—*what was up with that?*—he disappeared in a puff of smoky ash and I was left lunging at Kevin, still holding the stake in his hand.

"Don't even think about it."

I backpedaled, forcing myself to ignore the hunger even though he smelled so sweet, so *edible*. "I'm ravenous," I said, my voice sounding weak even to my own ears. "Nothing to drink since lunch."

"Learn to live with it," he said brusquely. "Try to take a nibble off me, and I'll stake you without even hesitating. And I really like you, Beth."

I could tell from the heat in his eyes that he meant it. The liking me part . . . and the staking me part as well.

"Oh, man," I said, sinking down to sit on one of the porch steps. "I was so angry and hungry I almost bit that guy." The hunger evaporated as questions filled my head. "Why was a vamp attacking me, anyway? And what would have happened if I'd bit him? Would I have screwed myself out of ever being human again?"

"Think, Beth," Kevin said, sitting down next to me. "You have to drink from *living* flesh. Vampires aren't alive. Nothing personal," he added with a nod to me. "But—"

"Sucking on him wouldn't mess me up. I get it." That was good to know. What *wasn't* good was that there was some nutty vampire out there who wanted me dead. I thought about the other attacks. Maybe there were even two or three vampires . . .

The thought gave me the creeps. Which, in my current undead state, was saying a lot.

He scooted closer to me. "You okay?" He turned so that he was facing me, our knees brushing. And as he shifted, something between us shifted, too.

"Yeah. I'm just. You know . . ." I trailed off, my brain having turned to mush.

Maybe it was the way he was looking at me, with his eyes dreamy and hungry all at the same time. Or maybe it was the way he touched me, his fingers curling gently into my hair. All I knew was that if I were alive my heart would be pounding double-time in my chest. As it was, my blood was doing that tingle number.

Then he leaned closer and kissed me, and it wasn't only

my blood that was tingling, it was my lips, too. Along with a few other nether regions.

He pulled me closer, one hand stroking my back and the other curling into my hair. I pressed against him, my head filled with the rather unfathomable fact that I was kissing a college boy. More specifically, a college boy was kissing *me*.

Me.

Beth Frasier, the girl most likely to not land a college boy. But there he was and there I was, and he obviously liked me. He liked me even though I was smart and wasn't popular. Heck, he liked me even though I happened to be a vampire.

Wow.

The situation was amazing. Heart-stopping. Wow-inspiring.

There was, in fact, only one thing wrong with it.

Clayton.

My head was filled with him. I couldn't stop thinking about him. It was like I was obsessed or something, and I did *not* want to be obsessed. I didn't want to be thinking of him.

Why should I be having Clayton thoughts, anyway? Clayton had dumped me. That wasn't exactly a relationship I needed to be mourning.

"Is this okay?" Kevin asked, pulling gently away from my mouth. "You're not—"

"Fine," I said, banishing all Clayton-related thoughts. "This is fine. Good. No, it's *great*. Yes," I confirmed. "Great is what it is."

His grin was slow. "Good," he said, and then he kissed me again, dispelling my secret fear that the first kiss had been the result of him falling and tripping on my lips.

I closed my eyes and tried to enjoy it. Tried not to think about Clayton. Tried not to think about the fact that I was a vampire and Kevin was a hunter.

Tried . . . and pretty much failed.

What was it that Clayton had said that afternoon? That he'd seen me kissing Kevin? Well, let him get an eyeful now!

I deliberately kissed Kevin back. Because I *hadn't* kissed him back earlier. Clayton had assumed that if Kevin's lips were on mine then I must have been kissing him, too. Never once did he ask if maybe he'd spied us at the exact wrong moment. If maybe Kevin liked me more than I liked him.

Well, *fine*. Served him right. No way was I staying loyal to a boyfriend who didn't want me. That's the kind of thing they talk about in health class, in the chapter on bad relationships. And I'm *so* not ending up as a guest on the *Jerry Springer Show*.

Kevin broke the kiss and stroked my hair. "Hey there," he whispered. "Where are you?"

Julie Kenner

I blinked, shoving down guilty boyfriend thoughts. "I'm here," I said. "I'm right here."

"I had the feeling you were far away," he said, with a gentle tap to my head. "In here."

"Oh. Right. No. I'm here," I assured him. "With you." I frowned a bit. "Actually, why are you here?"

"Not happy to see me?"

"Believe me. I was thrilled to see you. But again I ask . . . why?" Surely he hadn't come for smooches. Had he?

"I figured out who was after you the other evening. Not a vampire hunter."

"A vampire," I said. "That's old news."

"It wasn't when I got here."

"True." I leaned forward, resting my elbows on my knees. "You told me Clayton sent the hunter. Are you saying he didn't?"

Here was my chance to get confirmation that Clayton wasn't out to kill me. But if there was too much eagerness in my voice, I don't think Kevin noticed.

"Don't know. He could still be behind this."

"Oh." So much for confirmation.

"Sorry, Beth. But he could simply make a suggestion to another vampire whose interests are in line with his own."

"What do you mean? Clayton's the only vamp I've made. So why would any other vamps care about me?"

"The vampire war, of course."

"Um, hello? What are you talking about?"

"Warring vampire clans, of course. You're in the crossfire."

"*Ohhhh,*" I said. "Of course. Because sixteen-year-old newly turned vamps are always stuck in the middle of huge vampiric wars. Gee," I said. "I should have thought of that myself."

He made a face, apparently not appreciating the depths of my sarcasm. "The vamp population is essentially divided into two camps. You have the more modern thinkers, and then you have the traditionalists."

"Okay," I said. "And that means what to me?"

"The modern ones are like the folks you've met in school. The fact that they even *go* to school is evidence of that. Why should they even bother?"

"Steady stream of lunch?" I suggested.

"Yeah, well there is that. But they could find lunch in a park. No, these modern vamps want to move in the world. They want human things."

"Like cheerleading and football," I said, seeing where he was going with this.

"Right."

"And the other camp? I'm guessing they're more like right-wing conservative vampires?"

He laughed, but nodded. "That about sums it up. The other camp wants to keep the vampiric traditions alive. Moving in the dark. Living at night. Keeping their own company. From their perspective, humans are only good for food. Mingling with humans—even as a means to an end—really doesn't sit well."

"Got it," I said, wondering vaguely how it was that Kevin knew all of this. Considering he wasn't a vampire, he sure was tuned in to the vampire way of life. At the moment, though, I wasn't concerned about the source of his knowledge. I was interested in only one thing: what that knowledge meant to me. So I asked. "Why am I in the crossfire? I couldn't care less how the old-fashioned vamps want to live their lifes. It's not like I'm trying to stop them. Heck, I don't even want to *be* them, any of them."

"Honestly, Beth, you may be a brain, but there are times when you're completely clueless."

I raised my eyebrows and stared him down. "Excuse me?"

"I simply mean that it's obvious why you're their target," he said. "You're the one trying to solve the formula."

"The daywalking formula?" I asked. "But . . . but . . . but . . . It's not like I'm actually going to do that. So far, I don't have a clue."

"Apparently they've got more confidence in you than you have."

A million thoughts scrambled through my head. "But why try to kill me? Then they'll never have the formula. And what vampire doesn't want to walk during the day?"

"A traditional one," Kevin said. "With traditional vampire values."

"Talk about living in the past," I grumbled. "These guys are aware that we're well into the second millennium, right?"

"I'm sure they've made note of it."

"And you?" I asked, cocking my head so I could get a good look at his face.

"I'm well aware of what year it is, too."

I laughed. "I meant what do you think? About the formula?"

He brushed my lip with the pad of his thumb, making me feel all tingly again. "I have every confidence in you, too."

"Oh," I said, since that was about the only word my brain could process at the moment. "Oh."

And then he was kissing me, and my brain fizzled even

more, unable to process anything beyond lips and kisses and a vague image of Clayton's face, his green eyes watching me and a crooked smile playing at his cute mouth.

I pulled away from Kevin, more than a little freaked.

"You okay?"

"Fine," I said. Except that I couldn't keep thoughts of my ex-boyfriend out of my head while kissing my potential new boyfriend. Not good. Really not good.

But so like me. Wasn't I exactly the type to always want what I couldn't have? Jenny would say so, that much I knew for sure.

I sat there on the porch steps and tried to channel my best friend. *You can't have Clayton,* she'd say, *because he's not only dumped you, but there's still the slim possibility he's turned homicidal. So naturally, you want him more than ever. Get over it, Beth. College boy! Cute college boy. Cute college boy who saved your life. What do you need? An engraved invitation?*

"Right you are, Jenny," I whispered.

"Excuse me?"

I took the plunge and kissed him hard. After a few moments of superior kissing activity, he pulled back, his grin wide. "I'll repeat," he said. "Excuse me?"

I laughed, then sat up straighter. If I'd been breathing, I

would have taken a deep breath for courage. As it was, good posture would have to do. "Do you want to go with me to the Winter Dance? It's a high school thing, so if you don't, I understand, but—"

"I'd love to."

"Really?" I shifted a little, feeling pleased and shy.

"Absolutely."

"Oh. Well. Okay then." He reached over and took my hand, squeezing my fingers. I squeezed back, my happiness mingled with a sense of loss. Clayton was the one I'd wanted to go to the dance with. But life can change on a dime, and the only way to survive is to go with the flow. *That*, I'd learned the hard way.

Chapter 20

Kevin and I engaged in a little bit more smoochiness on the back porch. Not only was I trying to assuage my thinking-about-Clayton guilt, I was also working up to asking him to whack Nelson and put an end to the Nelson Fuller vamp factory. He might be a hunter and all, but that seemed like an awfully big request.

Apparently not so big to him, though. When I asked, he just shrugged. "For you?" he said. "Not a problem."

O-kay.

Considering I was now officially dating a college boy who would jump to my every command, my mood when I finally went inside wasn't nearly as upbeat as you'd think. Smooches with cute guys aside, I was still having a pretty crappy week.

I'd killed my boyfriend (more or less), almost been killed *by* my boyfriend, been the subject of boyfriend gossip, been threatened by the head cheerleader and a brainless jock, rejoined the cheerleading squad, and then I'd learned that I was stuck in the middle of some intense vamp warfare.

And as if that weren't enough, my stomach was rumbling so hard I needed a muffler, and my dinner plans were still in the hospital, well guarded under lock and key.

Wasn't that peachy?

At least I knew one thing for sure: it couldn't get any worse.

I was sitting at the kitchen table feeling sorry for myself when my mom came home, an event that pretty much signaled the coming of the apocalypse since it was before two in the morning.

"Beth," she said, her eyebrows shooting sky-high as she waltzed in through the back door. "What on earth are you doing up so late? Studying, I hope."

"Sure, Mom," I said. "I'm totally down with the studying." I scowled and looked down at the tabletop, waiting for her to grill me. My mom's a trial attorney, and she doesn't miss a trick.

Or, at least, she'd never missed a trick before. The Mom I knew and loved (despite all her freakish quirks) would have immediately latched on to the fact that I was sitting in a dark kitchen without a single book. Not exactly prime study conditions, if you know what I mean.

Tonight's Mom, however, didn't say a word. She just aimed herself straight for the coffeemaker. She poured herself a cup that had probably been brewed twenty-one hours before, took a sip, made a face, and then sat down at the table across from me.

"Actually," she said, "I'm glad you're awake. There's something I need to talk to you about."

"Ah," I said. "Okay." I frowned, worried because my mom wasn't exactly famous for her warm, fuzzy mother-daughter convos. Had she figured out my secret? Was she going to ground me? "What's up?"

She slid into a chair and folded her hands in front of her at the table, the height of professionalism. I had the sudden urge to look behind her to see if her secretary was there, taking notes. "I've been offered a new position at the firm," she said. "An excellent position, actually."

"Oh." More frowning on my part because this was so of the what-does-this-have-to-do-with-me variety. "Um, congratulations."

"Thank you."

"What does this—"

"The job's in Paris," she said at the exact same time, and since that statement pretty much trumped anything I was going to say, I closed my mouth, which had immediately fallen into an unattractive gaping-open position.

"Oh." I seemed to be saying that a lot in this conversation. "Oh. Um . . ." I'm sure there were a million questions I should have been asking, but somehow none of them came to mind. Until, "Are we moving to Paris, then?" *That* I said with a bit of a happy tone. Because even as I spoke the words, I realized what a good thing that could be. Bye-bye boyfriend problems and irritating assassins. Bonjour, Eiffel Tower, Notre Dame, and the Sorbonne.

An escapist fantasy, maybe, but I could live with it.

Of course, I'd have to figure out the little details of getting to France without getting stuck in the sunlight, but surely that was doable. If I suggested to Mom that I went a few days after her, then maybe—

"No, Beth," she said. "You'll be staying here. Your father and I talked about it. You'll be moving in with him."

Kerthunk.

Or, rather, *kablooey*!

Live with my dad? *So* not acceptable!

"No way," I said. "I can't—you can't expect me to—but you hate Daddy! How can you shove me off on him?"

Okay, that was totally playing the parental guilt card, but I could hardly share my real concerns with my mother. Like the fact that my dad lived in one of the downtown loft apartments. And I'd be sleeping in a pullout bed in a sectioned-off area with *absolutely no windows*. Good for the sun issue. Bad for the sneaking-out thing.

And as for that, how was I going to work my already complicated life? My father might be mostly clueless, but he's still a father. And fathers are notoriously overprotective of their little girls. Which meant that staying out late—on nights I wasn't at the hospital—would *so* not happen!

And I'd bet a million dollars he'd never let me date a college boy.

"You're ruining my life," I howled. "Mom, you totally can't do this!"

She was still sitting at the table, her face completely impassive. "First of all, I do not hate your father," she said. She tilted her head to the side and rolled her eyes. "I dislike the man intensely at times, but that's for reasons between your father and me and has nothing to do with his skill as a parent."

I must have made some sort of snorting sound because she shot me a dirty look.

"Second, I'm only going to be gone for three months. I

put up with the man for over sixteen years. I think you can manage ninety days."

"Mom—"

"And finally, there is no way that I'm pulling you out of class at this critical point in your education. College, Beth. That has to be where your focus is. After you've received your admission letter from Harvard, we'll celebrate with a trip to Paris. Until then, you need to concentrate on your schoolwork."

"But—"

"No buts, sweetie. The decision's already been made."

"Glad to know you were so interested in my input," I said snarkily.

The tone was not lost on my mother. She pointed to my room. "Go. We'll talk more tomorrow."

I bit back another nasty comment and went. That was best. Considering how irritated I was—and how hungry— my body screamed to actually bite my mother. I figured I was getting off easy by merely biting back a nasty comment.

As soon as I was in my room, though, I started hurling things. Stuffed animals, mostly, because I didn't want my mother to hear. Break something, and I'd get The Lecture. And I really wasn't up for that.

Live with my dad. *Live with my dad?*

That was a teenage girl vampire's nightmare.

I stalked around my room, trying to decide if there could possibly be an unluckier girl in all of the universe. I decided not to think about it, though. Because every time I thought about how bad my life had become, it seemed to take a turn for the worse. And I couldn't live with myself if I brought about the apocalypse.

Chapter 21

My alarm went off at 4:45 in the morning, and I groaned. Vamps are nocturnal, after all, and I'd barely fallen into a sound sleep. This switching of the internal clock simply so I could go to school was really a pain in the butt.

Even in my prevamp days, I was never an early riser, and I stumbled groggily toward the little refrigerator I'd hidden in my closet. Then I remembered that the little refrigerator was empty.

So not a beautiful morning.

I groped my way into my clothes and then out into the kitchen, where my early-bird mother greeted me with a cheery wave and an offer of coffee. I desperately needed the caffeine, but unless it was in blood, I couldn't keep it down.

I managed some sort of negative response, then sank into one of the kitchen chairs and banged my forehead on the table. Maybe if I banged hard enough the pain in my head would overshadow the empty stranglehold in my tummy.

"Honestly, Beth, if you can't be more pleasant in the morning, perhaps you shouldn't schedule these early morning activities."

I looked up at her, realized I was going to be breakfasting on my mom if I didn't get out of there, and grabbed my backpack.

I found Jenny in the driveway, the car engine idling as she listened to some Broadway sound track I didn't recognize.

"What are you doing here?"

She held a brown paper sack out to me through the driver's side window. "Breakfast. From the butcher shop. I already laced it with a package of Vivarin."

I'm pretty sure my eyes about popped out of my head, and when I opened the bag and saw the Styrofoam cup filled with fresh blood, I nearly dropped to the ground and wept tears of joy. Metaphorically speaking, anyway.

"I love you," I said.

"What are best friends for?" She nodded toward the passenger side. "Let's roll. We need to get you inside before sunrise."

The school isn't actually open before sunrise, but right after I'd changed, Clayton and I had told Ms. Shelby that we were working on the layout of the Christmas issue of the *Liberator*, and that we wanted to come in before school to get more work done. Since we're both editors on the paper and on the honor roll, she didn't even bat an eye. She swore us to secrecy and gave us a key.

Easy-squeazy.

It meant getting up insanely early, but at least my transcript wouldn't be overflowing with unexcused absences.

Interestingly, the vampire-jocks always managed to get to class, too, although most of them tended to blow off the early morning classes. That had always baffled me. Because *how* were they getting in? If they drove to school after sunrise, they somehow had to get from the parking lot to the building. How?

The only thing I could figure was that they were actually holing up somewhere *in* the school. For all I knew, they'd fed on their parents and then hid somewhere in the basement, stereotypically lined up in rows of gleaming coffins. Or maybe camped out in a bunch of REI sleeping bags.

The point being, I didn't know. But maybe if I could figure it out, I'd be one step closer to finding my maker.

"So are you asleep or what?"

I turned to Jenny, who cleared her throat meaningfully.

"Sorry. I'm tired and cranky and distracted." I held up the now-empty cup of blood. "But this was a huge help. Thanks. I can't believe you got my e-mail." I'd e-mailed a summary of my whole sucky day—including Kevin-lust and Cary's horrible no-more-blood announcement—right after I'd changed into my pajamas. Considering how late that had been, I couldn't believe she'd read it.

"Couldn't sleep," she said. "I was up thinking about ways to make my best friend human again, which hopefully includes a personality and a smile."

Okay, she had me. I broke down and laughed. "Okay, you win. I'm a total moron who doesn't deserve to have you as a best friend. Better?"

"Much," she said with a perky smile. "Glad you're not as grumpy anymore."

"So did you make any progress?"

"Um, hello? Don't I get the Kevin details?"

"Later," I said. "Maker. Mean vampire. Saving my hide? Ring any bells?"

"Right. Sure. As for progress, I guess that depends on your definition of progress. What do you want first? The good news or the bad."

"Ugh," I said. "Why does there always have to be bad?

How come no one ever asks if you want the good news or the really good news?"

"So do you want the good news or the really good news?"

"*Is* there really good news?" I asked suspiciously.

"Nope. I'm only trying to help your mood."

I slunk lower in my seat. "Don't bother. Just tell me."

"I took the photo files home over the weekend and I organized everything. And I've got a list of five teachers that I never saw outside."

"Well, that's good, right?"

"Yeah," Jenny said, "until you factor in the not-so-good news."

"Oh. What's that?"

"I poked around on the Internet, and I found some fan fiction. You know, stuff folks write online about vamps and stuff."

"Okay? So?"

"So there was this story about how some vamps can go out during the day if the moon is out, too. You know those weird days where you can see the moon in the sky even though it's totally sunny?"

"I know them," I said. "But a story on *the Internet*? That's your great resource?"

"Not exactly," she said, even as I watched her cheeks turned beet red.

"What then?"

"I, um, called Clayton's grandpa."

"Oh." I tried to decide how I felt about that, then decided it was okay. Save myself, and Clayton's saved, too. If Gramps could help us, then yay, Gramps.

I took a deep breath. "So who's on the list?"

"Coach Benson, Mr. Jordan, Mr. Tucker, Ms. Shelby, and Principal Dawson."

"Who's Coach Benson?" I asked. The only coach I knew of was Coach Dunne.

"*Assistant* coach," she said. "And aren't cheerleaders supposed to know that kind of stuff?"

"Don't remind me," I muttered grumpily.

"So what do you think? About the list?"

I gnawed on my lower lip, trying to think. "Well, I think we can rule out Ms. Shelby. I've known her too long, you know? And I'm sure I've seen her outside. At least, I think I have." I frowned, trying to remember. "Yeah," I said. "We've gone to the printer's during the day before. I know we have."

"Okay," Jenny said. "I'll cross her off. The rest?"

"Mr. Tucker is hardly the wild and wacky vampire type.

He's old enough to have been around even without being vamped. And he's . . . well, he's just Mr. Tucker."

"Hardly a rousing argument against vampiness."

"I guess."

"You know he likes you. If he was picking someone to be a vamp, I bet he'd pick you," Jenny said.

"Except the reason I was picked was because of my science smarts. Mr. Jordan makes *way* more sense."

"That's true," Jenny said. "And he's been way, way, way cool about letting you work in the chem lab during all your off periods."

"And writing me notes when I work there during my *not* off periods." I cocked my head to the side, considering. "He's a good bet," I said. "Yeah, he's a really good bet."

"Better than the others?"

"Who's left?"

"Coach Benson and Principal Dawson," she said.

"They're both technically assistants," I said, since Principal Dawson was actually Assistant Principal Dawson, but that's too much to say if you bump into him in the hallway. "If either one is some big, important vampire master dude, do you think he'd be willing to come to a high school and be some mortal's assistant?"

"It's a good cover, though," Jenny said. "And we know that the jocks are into becoming vamps."

"So the coach makes sense," I said. "Yeah, you're right."

"So what do we do?"

"We don't have a choice," I said. "We've got to test them all."

"Test?" she said, her eyebrows rising. "Like with holy water and stuff?"

"No, with the SATs. Of course with holy water!"

"But how? And what if none of them react to the holy water? If the outside during a moonlit day thing is true, the maker could be any other teacher."

She was right. There was no way to know if a daylight picture was taken when the moon was out with the sun. And if that little bit of folklore was true, it may be that the maker made it a point to be snapped on that particular day.

"We test the indoor dudes first," I said. "If none of them pan out, then fine, we move on." I paused. "Except . . ."

"What?"

"Test Ladybell, too."

"But I have pictures of her outside during the day."

"Could you see if the moon was in the sky?"

"Do you really think—?"

I looked out the window. "I don't know. But the cheerleaders know what's going on. And they're awfully keen on staying young and pretty. And Ladybell sure wants that cheerleading trophy. I think she should move onto the A list."

"Right," Jenny said. "Okay. Well, this is good. At least we have a starting point." She parked the car, and we got out. "It could be worse."

That's when I looked up and saw Clayton standing on the sidewalk. "I think it just got worse."

Chapter 22

"Hey," I said, dragging the toe of my sneaker through the grass.

"Hey yourself."

Jenny cleared her throat. All around, the moment was entirely lacking in comfort.

"Not that it hasn't been fun standing here chatting," I said, "but I'd really like to get inside before someone jumps out of the bushes and tries to kill me."

"Beth—"

I held up my hand to shut him up. "Don't even start," I said. "I'm going inside."

"I'm going with you."

I sighed. "You know what, Clayton? Don't. I . . . I don't think I can handle it, you know? Seeing you, I mean."

"Dammit, Beth! I'm trying to say I'm sorry!"

I squinted at him. "About what? Breaking up with me, or trying to kill me?"

"I didn't try to—"

I held up a hand. "Fine. Whatever. I believe you." I tilted my head back and forth. "Or, at least, I want to believe you. But I *heard* you. What was I supposed to think?"

"How should I know? I don't even know what you heard." He was right in my face, and I could feel the anger and the hurt flowing off of him.

"You!" I snapped. "Talking about how it hadn't worked and so you'd have to try again. But not by your grandfather's place because you didn't want him to know what was going on. What?" I said, poking him in the chest with my finger. "Were you ticked off that he was willing to let me live?"

His entire body seemed to sag. "I can't believe you really think I'd want you dead."

"You want to be human again, don't you?"

He tilted his chin up and looked me straight in the eyes. "Kill you," he said, "and I might be alive again. But I would *never* be human."

I blinked, trying to make sense of his words.

"Oh, wow," Jenny said, with her hand over her heart. "That is so romantic."

I held up my hands. "Wait, wait, wait. You broke up with me, remember? You *dumped* me!"

"I was pissed off. Come on, Beth. You were totally pulling my chain. But I haven't been able to stop thinking about you, and I figured maybe it's time for me to stop being mad. One of us had to make the first move."

"Oh," I said. And then, happier, "Oh!" Not that my happiness hung around all that long. How could it, what with the guilt settling in and squeezing out the possibility of any other emotion?

"Clayton, I'm so sorry that I doubted you even for a millisecond. It's just that, well, I killed you. I couldn't believe that you weren't a little bit mad. And I felt so guilty. And I knew that all you had to do was kill me to get back to normal. And right after that guy attacked me outside your grandpa's trailer park, I heard you—" I cut myself off, blinking. "Come to think of it, if you weren't talking about having me killed, what *were* you talking about?"

"Your birthday," he said. "We started going out after your birthday, and I felt bad about missing your sweet sixteen.

So I wanted to rent a limo and have it come by and surprise you. Only some of the plans got messed up, and then I figured that Gramps would think I was a romantic idiot, and so I—"

"Clayton," I whispered. I'd heard everything he said, but I'd stopped processing after "limo." I'd moved closer, and somehow his arms had gone around me. I started to feel all warm and tingly.

"Hey there," he said and kissed my earlobe.

"Hey." I snuggled closer. "But I kept seeing you. You've been watching me. You were outside my house." I froze, suddenly wondering if he'd been outside my house *last* night. Had he seen Kevin?

I stiffened, guilt shooting through me like hot sparks.

"You told me in my grandpa's trailer that someone had tried to kill you," he said. "I wanted to protect you. But since you obviously didn't want me around, I was trying to stay out of your way and keep you safe at the same time."

"That's so sweet," I said, starting to melt again, thoughts of Kevin evaporating as the heat Clayton and I were generating ramped up between us.

"Uh, guys?" Jenny said. "This is all very warm and snuggly, but sunrise?" She pointed to the horizon and the first glow of sunshine. Beneath my fingers, Clayton's skin glowed. That wasn't heat we were generating; that was combustion.

I looked at Clayton, and he looked right back at me.

"Run," he said, and we sprinted for the school.

Chapter 23

Kissing is technically not allowed in the halls of Waterloo High. That kind of behavior can totally get you detention. If you're caught, a teacher can write you up. A letter could be sent home to your parents.

A big red note could be stapled into your permanent record.

Clayton and I were *so* not caring. Or, rather, I cared a little bit about the permanent record part, but his lips . . .

Oh, how I'd missed those lips.

"I'm so sorry," I said when I came up for air. Which, as a vamp, is totally metaphorical since breathing was so not a necessary part of life anymore. Vampire kisses can go on and on. It's pretty cool, actually. Especially from the point of view of those participating in the kiss.

"You already said that," he reminded me. "About seventeen times now, I think."

"It bears repeating," I said. "Because it's true."

"I missed you," he said. "I was royally pissed at first, thinking you'd believe I'd do something like that, but then . . ."

"Then what?"

"I realized you were suffering from temporary insanity. And besides, you'd never turned anyone into a vamp before. I guess it was fair that you didn't know how I'd react."

"You are the coolest." Wasn't he the absolute coolest?

"Are we going to class or staying here and making out?"

"I vote for staying."

He laughed. "Actually, I do, too. But even so, I think we better go to class. Grades. College. That whole thing."

"Oh, sure. Spoil my fun."

He took my hand, and we started walking in the direction of something remotely academic. I knew I had classes in the building, but operating under the influence of lust like I was, I really couldn't remember what or where.

As we walked, we garnered a few stares, one or two points, and absolutely no catty comments. Considering I'd recently experienced the joy of nasty notes on my locker,

I thought the lack of stones from the villagers worth mentioning.

"Yeah, well, we're old news."

"We are?" I'd never really been news at all before. Even though the attention hadn't been welcome, it still felt a bit disturbing to be tossed off so quickly. "Why?"

"Didn't you read the *Waterloo Watch* last night?"

"Um, no," I said, wondering what Jenny had neglected to tell me.

From the other direction, Nelson hurried along, head down, a big, ugly hoody-type sweatshirt pulled over his face. *He* got the reaction I'd been expecting for me and Clayton. Lots of finger-pointing. Tons of whispering. And even one girl who tossed a glob of gum his way.

"The *Watch* didn't actually name him," Clayton told me. "But it was clear enough. The whole article rocked. Talked about how someone was giving funny drinks to a lot of the kids at Waterloo. And how to beware of Bloody Marys."

"Really?" I said, trying to sound innocent.

"Yeah. The article never crossed the line into talking about vampires. But danger . . . well, that was definitely suggested."

"Well, what do you know about that?" I said, then realized I sounded remarkably like my grandmother.

169

"*I* know that whoever's behind that blog has some inside information."

"Hmmm."

Clayton looked sideways at me, but he didn't push. He did, however, smile. He'd figure it out soon enough—if he hadn't already—so I felt no guilt for keeping Jenny's secret.

"I really missed you," he said after we'd walked a bit further. "I can't believe all that's happened while we were apart."

"Feels like it's been months," I said. "Not a few days."

"I know." He squeezed my hand. "We'll still be able to see each other even once you go live with your dad, right?"

I'd told him about that whole fiasco earlier. Now, I nodded. "Yeah," I said. "But it's gonna be hard. Dads are notoriously not on board with letting their teenage daughters go out at night. He's already talking about switching to a day shift so that he'll be more available to me."

"Maybe it won't be a problem."

"How can it not be a problem?"

"If you figure out the formula, we can go out during the day."

"That's a big 'if,' " I said. "I'm pretty much stuck. I'm hoping I learn something from Cary's DNA run, but if I don't get a break there, I'm running out of ideas."

"You'll think of something," he said. "Or maybe we'll find your maker, and then we'll both be human again. You can live anywhere. Windows, no windows. And you'll be able to go outside anytime."

"Wouldn't that be nice? But I wouldn't count the good fairy dust grains quite yet. Still, I'm looking forward to it in a perverse sort of way."

"How so?"

"I dunno." I scuffed my shoe on the polished floor. "I guess it's because I don't know my dad all that well, despite having known him for sixteen years. I figure this will be good for some daddy-daughter bonding."

"Will he still let you go to the Winter Dance?"

I focused on the still-scuffing shoe, wanting to neatly sidestep *that* touchy subject. "I don't know," I said. "But it doesn't matter. That's in a few days, and Mom won't have left for Paris yet."

"Oh. Cool, then. Because I wanted to ask you—"

The warning bell rang, and I started to pull away, dreading where this was going. "We need to hurry."

"This'll only take a sec. And we can get a tardy. No one will care."

"But—"

"Do you want to go with me?" he blurted. "To the Winter Dance? We could do the limo thing, since my first try at getting you a limo ride was a total bust."

Did I want to go? *Did I?* This was the boy I loved, after all, and I couldn't believe that I'd gone and made plans with some other boy simply because I'd had doubts about Clayton. *Stupid, stupid!*

Still . . .

I focused on my fingernails. Did the fact that I'd doubted Clayton mean that I didn't really love him? For a while, I'd been sure he was going to kill me. How could I have believed that of someone I loved?

I didn't know. All I knew was that I wasn't sure of anything anymore. Nothing, that is, except that I wanted to go to the dance with him.

"Beth? Are you running statistics in your head or something? Geometry proofs don't take this long."

"Sorry," I said, lifting my mouth to kiss his chin. I *did* love him. And I did want to go. And somehow, I'd figure this all out.

"Yes," I said. "Of course! I mean, duh! I'd love to go to the dance with you."

Chapter 24

"You didn't tell him about Kevin, did you?" Jenny asked, her voice rising with fear for my sanity.

"Shhh!" I raised a finger to my lips and looked around at the nearby lockers. Nobody was paying any attention to us, though. "Of course not!"

She pondered the ceiling with a little shake of her head. "Well, you can't go with both of them. You're going to have to uninvite Kevin."

"I know," I said mournfully. "I just don't know how." I thought of Larry Stein, who I'd technically been going with since eighth grade, since I hadn't had the guts to break up.

"Get over your wimpiness and figure it out," she said, in true drill-sergeant fashion.

"Right," I said. "Sure. I can do this. If it means I get to go with Clayton, I can do it." I checked out the area once more, this time using my vamp hearing to make sure no one was on the other side of the locker bank listening to us. All quiet. "Any news on Operation Daylight?" I asked, both because I was desperate to know and because I wanted to change the subject.

"It's not Principal Dawson," she said. "I had to spend all of first period pretending to paint a banner near the office, by the way, so I hope you appreciate my efforts."

"I do," I said. "But why were you painting?"

"Can of water for the brush," she said. "I had to spill it at the appropriate moment." She made a face. "Dawson wasn't happy. If he'd been a vamp, I think I might be dead now."

"Jenny," I said, suddenly fearful, "I can't let you keep doing this."

She waved off my fears. "No, it's okay. Really. I was mostly joking anyway."

I gave her *the* look. She cringed.

"Okay, so I wasn't joking, but now I'm smarter about it. I could have flicked some water from the paintbrush and waited to see if it smoked on his skin."

I scowled, because I knew I wasn't going to manage to

talk her out of continuing the testing. "At least we're making progress."

"Slowly," she said. "But we're getting there."

"Good," I said. "I don't know why, but it feels like we need to hurry. Every time I turn around, someone's trying to stake me. Sooner or later, they might manage it."

"We'll figure it out," Jenny said, giving my hand a squeeze. "I'll get close to Ladybell today or in the morning. I'll tell her I'm featuring her in my column or something."

"Fab," I said. "And I can easily do Tucker and Jordan."

"No," she said adamantly. "We talked about this. If you get some of the holy water on you accidentally . . ."

"It's not a big deal," I said. "Until I'm fully a vampire, it only makes me itch."

"Yeah, but the itch gets worse as time goes by, right?"

I made a face. "Yeah," I admitted.

"Well, what if it feels like fire ants? What if you accidentally get some on your face or hands and you itch so much they can tell that something is up before you have the chance to test them?" She shook her head. "No way. I'm your go-to girl. So let me do this. Promise?"

I wanted to argue, but she was right.

I promised.

Chapter 25

It was just as well I wasn't trying to nail Mr. Jordan with holy water, since he was totally absent from the chemistry lab. Pretty irresponsible of him, really, giving a junior full access after school hours.

I looked at Jenny and shrugged. "You might as well go and try someone else. I think he must have decided to take a date to dinner or something."

"It's dark outside," she said. "Maybe he was getting cabin fever."

"Maybe," I agreed. If so, I knew exactly how he felt.

"I'm totally striking out this afternoon," she said. "None of the teachers are where they're supposed to be."

"Tomorrow," I said. "That's the beauty of school. It keeps on coming."

She made a face. "And so do the midterms. Since there's no one around to douse, I guess I'll go home and study. Unless you want to come, too?"

I shook my head and waved her off. I hadn't heard from Cary with the DNA results. But even so, I was back in the lab trying to figure out the formula. Of course, since the sum total of my figuring involved me staring into space and waiting for a brilliant thought to strike, there wasn't a lot she could help me with. "Go forth," I said. "Learn things."

"I'll swing by the butcher shop and get you some blood first," she said, then headed out. I sat at one of the clunky lab tables, a copy of the daywalking formula spread out in front of me and a vial of blood in my hand. Inspiration did not immediately rush into the room. After an hour, I decided that inspiration obviously had somewhere else to be. I took a quick walk through the halls. When I got back, Clayton was waiting for me, along with a brown bag containing a care package from Jenny.

"Hey," I said, suddenly feeling shy.

"Hey yourself."

"Any progress?" he asked, pointing at the copy of the formula.

I glanced back at the lab table. "None. It's really beginning to tick me off."

"Can I help?"

I gestured to a chair. "You can try. Maybe we'll get lucky." I figured we had a shot. After all, Clayton's right behind me GPA-wise. If we couldn't figure it out between the two of us, we needed to rip up our National Merit certificates.

I called my mom to tell her I was staying at Jenny's, and called Jenny to clue her in. Clayton and I worked all night. We were still in the lab when morning came. We'd had absolutely no success. "Should we go to class?" Clayton asked.

"We can stay another hour or so," I said. "Mr. Jordan doesn't have any morning classes today."

"Cool," he said. "That gives us two hours to figure this out and finish up."

I rolled my eyes. "We might solve it," I said, then turned to a microscope as if to prove my point.

Beside me, Clayton continued to focus on the formula. "It's this 'intoxicates like wine' bit that's bugging me," he said. "I'm thinking you have to drink the formula."

"Ew," I said. But at the same time, I was perking up, my

head buzzing with new ideas. "Gross," I clarified. "But possibly correct." I'd been expecting that the formula would be slathered on, like suntan oil. I'd figured that made sense considering vamps can't drink anything that isn't blood. *That* I learned the hard way.

And then it hit me. "Blood!" I turned to Clayton, sure my eyes were shining. "It has to be blood! We *are* brilliant."

"Um, hello?"

"That's got to be the catalyst. The key ingredient. *Blood.*"

"Hate to rain on our parade," he said. "But vamps drink blood all the time. As far as I know, none of us is walking around in the sun."

"It's the language in the formula about the first of us. That's the key. The blood from when you're made a vampire."

"Your maker's blood?" His expression turned thoughtful. "But we drink that at the beginning. That's the whole point, right? Our maker's blood is what turns us."

But I'd already moved past that idea. "You're right. That's not it after all. No, the blood in the formula is our own. That's the blood you never drink, right?"

"So you're saying that the secret formula is simply drinking your own blood? And you got that from this?" he added, waving the translated Latin text in the air.

I put my hands on my hips. "Have you got a better idea?"

"Actually, no."

"We'll use me to test the theory," I said, holding up the vial. "I've got some of my blood right here."

He looked at the vial. "Are you going to drink it like that?"

"I think I'll mix something up," I said. "Just in case." I poured the blood into a clean beaker, then added some vitamin powder that I'd been using in my other experiments because it was heavy on the vitamin D. And because I could use the hit, I added some crushed-up Vivarin, too.

"Cheers," I said, holding up the beaker.

"I wish I could take you out for a real drink," he said. "Before the dance. We could go to Sixth Street and have a beer. Or champagne."

"We're not old enough to drink," I said.

"Moot point," he said, "since we'll never be old enough."

I put the beaker down and went to him. "Don't talk like that. We're going to find my maker."

He stroked my hair. "I know. I'm sorry. I'm tired. And it's going to sound silly, but I'm really looking forward to the dance."

I pulled away and started fiddling with some of the equipment I'd left sitting around on the lab table. "Oh? Why?"

"A normal date. Something not involving blood or secret formulas. We never got that, and I want that with you. Even if we will be mostly pretending."

"Me, too," I said, feeling guiltier by the second. I should have cut Kevin loose by now. I had his phone number. Why hadn't I called?

Because I'm a wimp, that's why.

"You should drink," Clayton said, oblivious to my mental flagellation. "Before the blood gets all clumpy."

"Ick." He was right, so I picked up the beaker. But I couldn't drink, despite the intoxicating scent that was, literally, making my mouth water. I had to ignore the hunger. I had to—

"I invited someone else to the dance," I blurted, then clapped my mouth shut. No, no, no! This was not the way to go about this! I was supposed to break it off with Kevin, and then Clayton need never know.

You thought he tried to kill you, a tiny voice said. *At the very least be honest with him now.*

I scowled, trying to decide if my conscience was really being my guide, or if it just figured it was easier to fess up to Clayton—who was both my friend and my boyfriend—than to admit to a college boy that I wanted to blow off a date with him.

"What?" Clayton said, his forehead creased. "What are you talking about?"

"When I thought you were trying to kill me. I asked someone else. I'm sorry!"

I saw the confusion pass over his face, and then I saw his features harden. I'd seen that expression before. I didn't much like it. "Oh," he said. "Who?"

"Kevin." I didn't meet his eyes.

"Ah." He ran his tongue over his teeth. "You know I don't really like Kevin, right?"

"I'm sorry," I whispered. "I thought . . . I didn't know . . ." I closed my eyes and counted to ten. "I wanted to go with you so badly. So when you asked me, I didn't think. I just said yes."

His face shifted and a smile lit his eyes.

"Should I back out? I can call and cancel." I moved closer, happy to feel his hand go to my waist. "I'll totally do it."

"Hell, yeah," he said. "No way some other guy is taking my girlfriend to the dance."

"Really?" I shivered as he stroked my cheek. "You do the honor-bound macho-guy thing really well."

"We're a couple now, Beth," he said. "Break the date."

I nodded, deliriously happy. So delirious, in fact, that I even felt capable of overcoming my wimpyness. A feeling that I hoped would last. Especially since—when I tried to call Kevin to do the deed right then—all I got was his voice mail. The moment of truth would come when he called me back.

And then Clayton kissed me, and I totally forgot all about the dance. Because I was kissing my boyfriend in the science lab and it felt so awesome.

Right then, I'd happily stay a vampire forever if it meant we could kiss like this forever. Because—

"Isn't that sweet?"

We broke apart, Nelson's voice having the same effect as a bucketful of very cold water.

He looked at the lab table. "Ah, liquid refreshment. Aren't you going to invite me to share?"

Clayton stepped in front of me in a protective-guy stance. Is he great or what?

"Oh, give it up, Clayton," Nelson said. "I'm not here to pummel either of you. I just want the formula. That's it, isn't it?"

I looked at Clayton, wishing I could read his mind. We *could* give it to Nelson. Even if we were on the right track, surely the blood thing was individual. Mine would work on me and me alone. Which meant Nelson would end up fried. A lovely thought, but probably too much to hope for.

Besides, what if it was just *any* vampire blood, and I'd whipped up a formula from scratch? Did we want to be responsible for Nelson the Daywalking Vampire? Personally, I didn't.

"We didn't make it for you," Clayton said. "Send your master down here, and we'll be happy to turn it over."

I widened my eyes. As plans go, that one was both bold and scary.

Nelson, however, wasn't impressed. He lunged across the room for the beaker. And because I *really* didn't want him having my formula, I lunged, too. I got to the beaker first and drank, managing to down about half of it before Nelson got to me.

He grabbed my arm, twisted it back at the wrist, and pried the half-full beaker out of my hand. "Bottoms up," he said, then drank, managing to swallow mere seconds before Clayton tackled him.

"Whoa there, boy," Nelson said, as Clayton pulled out a stake. "I don't think you can do that to me." As if as proof, the stake that Clayton had aimed at Nelson's chest burst into flames. "I, however," Nelson began, pulling his own stake out of a back pocket.

"No!" I screamed and lunged toward them. I knocked Clayton clear, then was about to land a kick on Nelson when he shifted, somehow managing to pick me up and hold me over his head.

This is the problem with being a girl, even a girl vampire. As much as I'd like to say that years of gymnastics and dance has made me strong enough to fight off obnoxious, pissed-off jock types, it really hasn't. At the end of the day, I'm still barely a hundred pounds, and I hit like a girl.

Right then, I was hitting like my life depended on it, which I think maybe it did. I'm pretty sure Nelson and I were on the same level, so I wasn't fearful that he'd stake me, but that only made me more scared. Because I didn't know *what* he was going to do.

"Let's test the formula," he said, rushing toward the windows, currently covered by posters of various molecules.

As Clayton hollered in protest, Nelson hauled me back and tossed me toward the glass. It shattered instantly, shards flying everywhere, the cacophony enough to practically burst my eardrums.

The chem lab is on the second floor, and I plummeted to the ground, expecting any moment to be immolated by the sun. I felt the heat of its rays on my face, the tingle of sunshine on my skin. I waited . . . and nothing happened.

It worked! My daywalking formula had worked!

I stood up, then brushed glass off my clothes. We were in

the middle of first period, so nobody was outside to see my impromptu exit from the building. I put my hands on my hips, tilted my face back to the sun, then looked straight back the way I'd come.

Nelson was standing there, gaping at me from a shadow near the window. So, for that matter, was Clayton.

"Time to go to the master," Nelson called down, with a thin smile. "I think he's going to want you to whip up a lot more of that cocktail."

"Yeah? Well, you're going to have to come and get me."

"Babe," Nelson said, "that's exactly my plan." And then he disappeared back into the lab. I had no idea where he'd gone, and I looked for Clayton, but he'd disappeared, too. Then I realized—Nelson had backed up for a running start. He jumped through the window, legs pumping as if he were running on air.

He took one look at me, let out a howl of victory, and then promptly burst into flames.

Chapter 26

"So it didn't work on Nelson because it wasn't his blood?" Jenny asked. We were in my bedroom, Jenny at my desk, and Clayton next to me on the bed.

"That's what we think," I said, looking at Clayton.

"Let's test the hypothesis," he said, then opened my desk drawer and found a box cutter in the back. And then, before I could yell out or anything, he sliced his palm.

"Clayton!"

"A test," he said, and then as Jenny and I looked on, he dumped out my pencil cup and let his palm drip blood into it. As Jenny and I gaped, he put the pencil cup to his lips and drank.

Can I just say, *ick*?

After a second, he looked at me. "Did you feel any different?"

I shook my head. "Nope."

"Maybe it worked then. I feel the same, too."

"So how do we test it?" Jenny asked.

"I know," I said. "The box." I'd rigged up a box not too long ago with a UV light in it. I'd designed it for this very thing—testing the daywalking formula. But I still wasn't crazy about the idea of using it now to burn my boyfriend's hands.

"It's not going to hurt me," Clayton said, apparently reading my mind. "You figured out the formula. It worked on you, so there's no reason that it won't work on me." He came over and gave me a quick kiss. "You're brilliant, Beth."

I managed a half smile, more from the compliment than any confidence I had in the experiment. "Whatever," I said.

I put the box on the bed and plugged it in. Clayton stuck his hand in and closed his eyes. "Okay," he said. "Go."

I held my breath, then turned it on. For a second, I thought it worked, and then Clayton's face contorted in pain. He scrambled to jerk his hand free. I scrambled to pull the plug.

"*Aggghhhh,*" he howled, clutching his burnt hand close to his body. "Damn, that hurts!"

"Let me see," I said, but he wouldn't let me get close to it.

"It'll be okay," he said. "A few nights and a few pints, and it'll heal."

I leaned my head on his shoulder. "That's true, thank goodness. But we still don't have an answer. Why me, but not you?"

"I don't know," he said, his face reflecting all the bafflement I felt.

"Maybe Kevin would have a theory," Jenny said. "He always seems to know vampire-type stuff like that."

Clayton's icy look was almost enough to freeze boiling water. "My grandpa would be a better one to ask."

Jenny held up her hands. "Right! Sorry!"

"And did you guys ever stop to think that maybe Kevin's the one behind all the attacks on Beth?"

"No way," I said. "He saved my butt."

"He was there," Clayton said. "Conveniently there for the attacks. At least he was there for the last two. So of course he was in the proper place to save you."

"I—" I shook my head. "No. No way. You're being jealous. He's a vampire hunter. He's not working with the vamps. His job is to stake them."

Clayton looked me straight in the eye. "He didn't stake you," he said. And all I could do was swallow.

"Anyway," Clayton went on, "I know I'm a little biased against the guy, but he does seem to know a lot. And you did say that he told you specifically to trust no one."

"Yeah," Jenny said. "But that didn't mean *him*."

"Didn't it?" Clayton asked. "If this were a movie, he'd totally turn bad in the third act. And then we'd all feel like idiots for not understanding that the 'no one' included himself."

"It's not a movie," I said. "And even if it were," I added, with a meaningful kiss, "it's a romance. *Not* a horror film."

Or so I hoped, anyway.

Chapter 27

I walked the two of them out, said good-bye on the back porch, and when I came back in I found my father sitting at the kitchen table.

"I . . . oh. Hi." I squinted at him. "When did you get here?"

"A few hours ago," he said. "I was unpacking in the bedroom. Didn't want to disturb your study session."

"Ah." I twisted a strand of hair around my finger, wondering if he'd overheard any of our "study session."

"There's coffee," he said, pointing to the counter.

"No thanks." My stomach revolted at the mere thought. "Um, don't take this the wrong way, but why are you here?"

He chuckled. "Your mom asked me to come stay through

the weekend. She had to fly to Paris to set some things up. We thought it was easier for me to stay here than to move you into the apartment, since it's only for a few days this time."

"Oh. Right." I smiled at my dad, the false, painted-on kind of smile. "Great to see you." *So* not true. I like my dad and all, but this was Winter Dance weekend. Really not the optimal time for father-daughter bonding. Especially since I had a boyfriend to consider. Not to mention a date with a college guy.

The thought of Kevin steeled me, and I slunk back to my room. I rummaged around in my desk until I found the card he'd given me with his number on it. I might be a wimp about canceling, but if I told him that I was back with Clayton, surely *he'd* do the canceling, and I'd be off the hook. Right?

He answered his cell phone on the first ring. "Hey, gorgeous. What's up?"

"I . . . oh . . . nothing much."

He laughed. "You're a terrible liar, Beth."

"Yeah," I said. "It's not one of my gifts."

"Seriously, why'd you call? Because I was going to call you tomorrow. I want to know what color your dress is."

"My dress?"

"For the dance," he said. "I want to get you a corsage that doesn't clash."

"A corsage?" I flushed to my toes. No one had ever given me flowers before. Except my dad, and he didn't count.

"Yeah. You know. Flower. Dance. It's a date thing."

"Right. Um . . ." I cleared my throat. "I haven't bought my dress yet. But when I do, I'll tell you." I hesitated. "If you still care, that is."

A pause on his end. "Okay, I'll bite. Why wouldn't I care?"

"Because I found out that Clayton wasn't trying to kill me?" I said it as a question, then closed my eyes, waiting for his response.

"Ah," he said. "I see."

"I'm sorry, Kevin. But he's . . . well, he's Clayton."

"Can't compete with a first boyfriend," he said. "I get that. Especially a boyfriend you have so much in common with." The last was said with a hard edge, and I flinched a little.

"I like you," I said. And the truth was, I meant it. He was cute and funny, and he'd saved my life. His kisses made me feel all tingly.

But I liked Clayton more. And I tingled around him all the time. Not only when his lips touched mine.

I heard his loud exhale. "So you're calling to cancel our date."

"Um, maybe. I guess." I took a deep breath, told myself I was a pathetic wimp, and nodded to my reflection in the mirror. "Yes," I said. "I am. I'm sorry, but he's the one I want to go with."

"I see," he said tightly.

"I'm sorry," I said, feeling like a jerk.

"Don't be sorry," he said.

"So you're not mad?"

"Nope," he said, although I'm not sure I believed him. "And you're not going to be mad when I try again, right?"

"Try again?"

"To get you to go out with me." His voice was low and sort of oozed through the telephone. I melted a little.

"No," I whispered. "I won't be mad."

"Clayton's a lucky guy."

"Thanks." I cleared my throat, thinking about what Clayton had said. About how he didn't trust Kevin. "Um, Kev?"

"What?"

"How come you didn't, you know, do anything about Nelson?"

"Because you beat me to it," he said.

"I'm serious."

"So am I," he said. "That's not the kind of thing I can rush. The kid was a high school student, vampire or not. I can't waltz into the high school and whack him. That could get a hunter noticed by the police. Or worse."

"Oh. Right. Sure." That made sense. At least, I thought it did.

"We good?"

"Sure," I said. "We're great."

"Okay," he said. And then he hung up.

Chapter 28

Time passes remarkably quickly when you're waiting for a dance. And that's true even if you're not wasting time doing nonsense like searching for daywalking formulas.

Not that I was totally off the clock vampire-wise. True, I hadn't been attacked in a few days (yay!) but we were still working to discover the identity of my maker. So far, though, Jenny wasn't having much luck in her quest to splatter our suspects with holy water. She did succeed in nailing Ms. Shelby and Ladybell, but the results were negative for both.

And while she'd been trying to test Mr. Tucker, Coach Benson, and Mr. Jordan, those suspects were more elusive.

Primarily because they weren't in school. Mr. Tucker was downtown at some classical education seminar, and no one knew where Mr. Jordan was. Coach Benson was at another high school, doing some scrimmage thing.

Not that the three potential stooges were my priority at the moment. Sure I wanted to kill my maker and return myself to humanity. But I had other things on my mind. Namely, finding the perfect dress.

Which was why Jenny and I were spending our evenings at the mall. She didn't have a date, but she said that didn't bother her since a real woman was comfortable accompanying herself to social functions. Maybe so, but a real woman still needed a real dress.

By Friday, we had the wardrobe down, and Jenny had given me a ride home so that we'd both have plenty of prep time before the dance. She poked around in my jewelry box, then pulled out a pair of dangly faux-emerald earrings. "These totally match my dress," she said, referring to the flouncy green vintage number she'd found in one of the shops on South Congress. "Can I?"

"Sure," I said.

She glanced at the clock. "I need to run if I'm going to make it home in time to change and do my makeup." She frowned. "We'll have fun, right? Even though I'm a total loser."

"What about uber-feminism?"

"Yeah, right," she said. "I'd rather have a date."

"It'll be a knockout evening," I said. "It has to be."

Chapter 29

At five forty-five, I was pacing in the living room. At five fifty, I heard a horn.

My dad looked up from the newspaper he was reading. "A horn? He's not coming to the door?"

"It's okay, Daddy," I said, which was a total lie. A *horn*? What kind of date was this? "He's got a sprained ankle," I said, adding to the lie. "I made him promise to honk."

My dad stared at the door, and for a second I thought he was going to challenge my lie. Then he nodded and pointed to his cheek. I gave him a kiss, and he told me to have a good time.

I hurried outside, arriving at the limo—which ranked a huge *wow* despite the totally rude honking thing—right as the driver stepped out. "Madam," he said, then opened the door.

I nodded my head, trying to act regal. "Thank you," I said, then gathered my skirts and bent down to enter.

As soon as I did, someone grabbed me around the neck and jerked me inside. I screamed, but the sound was muffled by the slamming door.

And then I felt the sharp prick of a needle sinking deep into my arm.

The world turned fuzzy, and as the pressure around my neck lessened, I looked up. "Clayton?" I said, blinking a bit to stop the world from spinning.

The dark face above me shook his head. "Forgive me for hijacking your dance plans," he said. "And allow me to introduce myself. I am Renault. And you, young lady, have been causing me no end of trouble."

Chapter 30

"Should have let me kill her! Tyrone got staked because of her!"

I tensed, consciousness coming slowly back to me. I kept my eyes closed, desperate to hear what was being said around me, and certain they'd all shut up if my eyes popped open.

Also, I needed time to come up with a plan. Because from the feel of things, I was crammed into a cage. A very small cage, where the cold, steel bars pressed against me on all sides.

"Tyrone was staked because he's a fool," a smooth voice responded. "And you deserve to be for the part you played in his foolishness. The two of you went after her against my direct orders." *Renault,* I thought, remembering the dark face from the limousine. "I never ordered a kill," he said, and I relaxed a little. "She needs to live until we get the information from her."

Oh. So much for relaxation.

"She'll never tell us," the other voice said, and murmurs of assent filled the room.

"Trust me, Arnaud, I assure you she will." Footsteps approached my cage. "Won't you, my dear?"

I tensed, and then I heard Renault laugh.

"Come on, Elizabeth. It's obvious you aren't asleep. Open your eyes and talk to me."

"Why should I?" I asked. "After I talk, you're going to kill me."

"Possibly," he said. "But depending on the answers, there may be no need to take your life."

I opened my eyes. "Yeah? Well, tell me what answers win me *that* lottery, and I'll be happy to share."

His mouth twitched. "I'd heard you would be challenging."

"You have no idea."

"Mmm."

"Let me kill her," Arnaud said, baring fangs.

I shrunk back as much as I could in my teeny-tiny cage.

202

That was when I noticed that they were all dressed in formal wear. Black pants. White shirts. The few women wore red gowns with low-cut bodices and tight corsets. And they all wore flowing black silken capes.

Since I had a feeling they weren't planning on crashing the Winter Dance, I had to figure that I'd been kidnapped by a group of traditionalist vampires.

"Read a little too much Bram Stoker?" I asked. "You'd blend in more in Hilfiger. Or even Old Navy."

"I assure you our ways are quite satisfactory," Renault said. "As is our wardrobe."

"Whatever. I guess the corset's not that big a deal to a vamp, anyway. Seeing as we don't have to breathe and all."

"*Please* let me kill her," Arnaud said.

"Be quiet," Renault said, his whispered voice allowing no argument. "As you undoubtedly have discovered, we approach our heritage from a more traditional standpoint. We believe in the beauty and majesty of our kind. We revere the royal family. We limit our interaction with the unclean humans. It is the way that all of our kind should live."

"Yeah, right," I said. "What royal family?"

He pursed his lips, his nostrils flaring. "The questions are mine to ask," he said. "Now tell me, have you interpreted the text? Have you successfully completed the formula?"

"No," I said, then clapped my hand over my mouth. I hadn't wanted to answer at all. What was going on?

"Drug," Renault said, as if I'd asked the question aloud. "It will wear off in an hour or so. Assuming you're still alive."

"Great," I said. "So glad y'all invited me to your little party."

"She *is* amusing," Renault said to Arnaud.

"Lucky us," Arnaud said. "Kill her, already."

"She's lying," came a voice from the back. A small, blonde female vampire stepped forward. "She has the formula. She's walked during the day."

"I do *not* have the formula," I said, keeping the image of Nelson firmly in my mind. My mouth wanted to answer the second part of the woman's statement and admit that I'd walked in the sun. That information, though, was sure to get me killed. And although it took all my strength, I managed not to say anything.

If the woman had asked a question, though, rather than simply making a statement, I'm not sure I could have fought the force of the drug.

"I don't have a formula," I repeated, which was completely true. I knew how *I* could walk in the sun. But the formula for the whole vampire population? *That* was still a mystery.

"She cannot lie," Renault said. "You all know the power of the drug."

More murmurs, this time of agreement.

"You are working on it, though?"

"Yes," I said. "I'm working on it."

"Do you believe you are close to solving the riddle of the formula?"

"I thought I was," I said. "But now I don't know."

"Why you?"

"I don't understand the question."

"There are rumors within the community," he said. "Rumors that you were made so that you could solve the riddle and discover the daywalking formula."

"Yeah," I said dryly. "I've heard those rumors, too."

"So I ask again. Why you?"

"I don't know," I said, and for the first time I was glad of that.

"Hmmm." Renault paced in front of me, his cape fluttering behind him. I used the lull in the questions to look around. The room was small and dark, but when I looked up, I thought I saw stars. A glass ceiling?

"Kill her," Arnaud said again. "If we kill this one now, they will be that much more hindered." He took a step toward Renault. "Obviously they think that she is the girl in the prophecy. The one who can bring about the completion of the formula. Kill her and be done with it, before this abomination is brought forth into the world."

I watched, terrified, as Renault made his decision. When he squared his shoulders, I cringed, certain I knew what was coming. "My compatriots were rash," he said, "seeking to kill you before we learned answers. The attacks were ill founded and stupid. For that, we apologize."

"Gee, thanks," I said, but with a tiny bit of hope. Why apologize to someone they were going to kill?

"Now, however," Renault continued, "we have learned the answers." I swallowed. "My companions are correct. It is time for you to die."

"I'm really not keen on the dying plan," I said, trying to scoot back in my cage, even though there was no place to go. "Couldn't I say I'd forget all this silly formula business, and we could let that be the end of that?"

"I'm afraid not," Renault said, pulling a large wooden stake from a pocket in his cape. "I'm sorry, my dear. The truth is, I rather like you."

"I'm flattered," I said. And then, as he lunged toward me, I screamed.

Above us, the ceiling shattered, the dissonance of breaking glass and wails of surprise drowning out my own cry.

Renault whipped around, temporarily forgetting me. And I cried out in joy as Clayton and Kevin—both dressed to the nines in tuxes—leaped from the broken ceiling into the middle of the fray.

My heroes had arrived.

Chapter 31

For two guys who didn't much like each other, they fought together like champs, taking out two of my captors within seconds of hitting ground. That surprised me, actually—how could Clayton kill vampires? But I realized that either my anonymous maker (and therefore me and Clayton, too) was *way* higher than them on the vamp family tree, or else they were in a different tree altogether. Vampire tribes? Could be, I guess. After all, Renault had talked about royalty.

Seeing their buddies turn into puffs of dust convinced most of the crowd to scatter, but a few stayed, determined to fight for the right to ensure that little old me ended up dead.

How nice to be the center of so much attention.

As Arnaud went for Kevin, and the mouthy female vamp

jumped Clayton, Renault turned his attention back to me, apparently wanting to make sure I was out of the picture no matter what.

"Clayton!" I screamed as Renault led with the stake.

Clayton heard me, and kicked the vamp he was fighting in the kneecaps. The girl collapsed in pain, and Clayton leaped toward me, grabbing Renault's cape at the last possible second. The stake scraped my dress, scarring the pink silk, but except for that minor fashion emergency, I was fine.

Clayton, however, wasn't. Renault was obviously an old vampire, with some serious strength, and it was taking all of Clayton's efforts to defend against his attacks.

"Kevin!" Clayton shouted, as I banged against the lock of my cage with my shoe. "Toss me the bottle."

"Are you sure?" Kevin asked, ducking to narrowly avoid Arnaud's punch.

"I've got a plan."

I had no idea what they were talking about, but watched in awe as Kevin—while using one hand to wield a defensive stake—reached into his jacket pocket and pulled out a large vial with a cross etched on it. *Holy water.*

And he was throwing it to Clayton?

Apparently so, because Clayton caught it, then poured it all over his still-burned hand. "Clayton!" I screamed.

"No feeling," he said, and then pressed his hand firmly against Renault's face.

The other vampire obviously still had all of his nerve endings, because his scream was loud enough to pierce heaven. And when Clayton took his hand away so that he could pull out a stake, Renault kicked him in the gut and then ran.

Clayton turned and raced toward Kevin, who was still going at it with Arnaud, the last of the vampires not to flee.

"Enough," Clayton said. "You guys kidnapped my girlfriend. Nobody does that and gets away with it." And then he grabbed Arnaud's arms and pinned them back, leaving the vamp's chest wide open for the stake that Kevin slammed home.

And then my two heroes were standing in front of each other, nothing but dust in the air between them.

"Good job," Clayton said, holding his hand out to Kevin.

"Right back at you," Kevin said.

They stared at each other in some sort of guy-bonding moment. I let it go on for about two seconds, and then I cleared my throat. "Hello? Damsel in distress here. You wanna get me out of this cage?"

Kevin slapped Clayton on the back, and they both headed over. It took a few minutes, but they managed to pry the door open. I crawled out, sore and cramped, but alive.

"I love you guys," I said, giving them both a hug. What I didn't say was that I really meant it. How could I not, with the drug still flowing through my veins? "I've never been happier to see anyone in my life."

"It was Clayton's doing," Kevin said. "I wouldn't have known anything was wrong if it wasn't for him."

"I called Kevin as soon as I realized what happened," Clayton said. "Once I learned that someone had already picked you up for the dance, I mean."

I winced. "My dad?"

Clayton waved away my fears. "Clueless. I promise. I made up a bullshit story about a senior class prank, and he totally bought it."

"But how did you know where to come?"

Kevin just smiled and looked at Clayton. "I make it my business to know what's going on in the vampire world. Keep informed, stay alive. That's my motto."

I gave Clayton a meaningful look, and he shrugged, properly abashed. "A good plan," he said. "Staying informed, I mean. It sure as hell paid off this time."

I laughed, then hooked an arm through each of theirs. "Gentlemen," I said, "care to take a lady to a dance?"

Chapter 32

"**D**id you see Tamara's face?" Jenny asked. "You getting out of a limousine with *two* guys. I thought she was going to turn bright green and grow roots right there."

"It was a Kodak moment," I agreed. I looked around the gym. "Where are my knights in shining armor, anyway?"

"Clayton went to get us punch," Jenny said. "I'm not sure about Kevin."

"There he is," I said, pointing toward the snack table. He was talking with Ladybell, standing a little too close, as if he was either flirting or trying to douse her with holy water. Considering this was Kevin we were talking about, I was guessing the latter.

"Did you tell him I'd already tested her?" Jenny asked.

"Yup," I said. "I caught him up completely during the ride here."

"I think Kevin's the type who likes to do that kind of thing himself," Clayton said, coming up from behind and handing us both little plastic champagne flutes of punch.

Jenny sniffed. "If he doesn't think I'm doing a good job, then he can test all of them himself."

"They're here?" I asked, perking up at the possibility of finding my maker tonight. And why not? So far it had been a vamp-o-rific night. Might as well go for the gold.

"All the teachers are," Jenny said. "Chaperones."

This would be like shooting ducks in a barrel. Between Kevin and Jenny, they could slap some holy water on Tucker, Benson, and Jordan, and in a flash I'd know which one was my maker. "So where are they?"

She frowned. "No clue. If it were me and I was chaperoning, I'd sneak out. If anyone caught me, I'd say I was going to the bathroom."

"You've given this a lot of thought," I said with a laugh.

She shrugged. "These things bear considering."

"What things?" Kevin asked, joining us.

"She's not a vampire," Jenny said, nodding toward Ladybell. Kevin looked confused.

"She's frustrated that you're double-checking her work," I explained, while Jenny huffed.

"I wasn't," he said. "Scout's honor."

Jenny crossed her arms over her chest. "Then what were you doing?"

"She spends too much time around vamps," he explained. "And around wannabe vamps. The cheerleaders and the jocks," he added, as if we needed an explanation.

"So?" Jenny asked.

"So I figure she's either a pet or she's under someone's influence."

"What do you mean?" Clayton asked, interested. "A pet?"

"Sure. Like the cheerleaders. They run around doing all the stuff the jock vamps want. They know the score, but they're helping anyway, hoping to get something out of it in the end."

"Do you think she is?"

"No," he said, shaking his head. "I think she's been glamoured."

My eyes widened as I took a step back. I'd thought about the jocks using a glamour to get kids to drink the master's blood and become vampires, but it had never occurred to me that the master might be using a glamour to have kids—or teachers—do vampirish things for them.

"Wow," I said. "You could be right."

"It makes sense," he said. "I've seen the effects of a long-term glamour before. She definitely has that glazed look about her."

I didn't bother to tell Kevin that Ladybell had looked glazed for years.

"Plus, it makes it safer for your maker," Clayton said. "She's got access to the cheerleaders and the jocks. They get orders from her, and she genuinely can't tell them the source."

"So Nelson and Tamara couldn't identify the maker for us even if they'd wanted to," Jenny said. "Damn."

Kevin nodded, frowning. "Unfortunately, knowing this doesn't help us much. If she doesn't know who's putting the glamour on her, we can't fight the information out of her. We'll need to go your holy water route."

"We don't have to," I said grimly. "I know who my maker is."

Chapter 33

"You're sure it's Tucker?" Jenny said as we all marched down the hall toward the Latin classroom.

"Yeah," I said. "I'm sure."

Kevin had made a sidetrip to his car, and now he had a crossbow slung over his shoulder, making him look all the sexier in his tux, I thought. The rest of us had stakes. Not that I could kill Tucker. But that didn't mean I wouldn't try.

"How can you be sure?" Clayton asked. "I thought Jordan and Benson were in the running."

"The assembly," I said. "I saw them talking. I didn't think about it at the time, but now . . ."

"Now it's clear that it was Tucker doing the talking and Ladybell doing the falling-under-your-spell routine?"

"Pretty much," I said.

"It makes sense," Clayton said. "The formula was in Latin, and he knows how good you are at it."

"And I got that warning e-mail after I pretty much told him I wasn't going to worry about my personal ancient text project." I made a low noise of frustration. "Argh! To think I actually *liked* him."

"Apparently he liked you, too," Kevin said dryly.

I shot him a not-so-nice look.

"Shut up, guys," Clayton said. "We're almost there."

We slowed to a crawl and walked softly down the hall toward the Latin classroom. The door was open, and Tucker was at the blackboard, writing out an assignment for Monday. "Come in, Elizabeth," he said, without turning around.

"Is it really you?" I said. "Are you really my maker?" My voice was cold, barely recognizable.

He turned to face me. And then he had the nerve to smile. "I am the one permitted to claim that honor, yes."

"You ruined my life!" I said.

"I brought you to your destiny," he responded. "For hundreds of years, I've known that this was my duty. You, Elizabeth. And I've done my duty well."

I shook my head, baffled.

"What is he talking about?" Clayton asked. "What are you talking about, old man?" He held up his stake.

Tucker just laughed. Which made sense because if Tucker was my maker, then Clayton couldn't stake him.

"Maybe *this* isn't so funny," Kevin said, holding up the crossbow.

"Good plan, Kevin," I said. "For that matter, I think I'd like to hire you to do a job for me." I looked meaningfully at Tucker. "Kill him. Give me my life back."

"Kill me, and you have no answers." He smiled at me, the anger in his face dissolving into kindness. "You have questions, yes?"

"Um, yeah." I glanced at my friends. *What was going on here?* Unfortunately, they looked as confused as I felt.

"Then take this opportunity to ask."

I hesitated, wondering if I was smelling a trap. Then I realized I didn't care. I had to know. "Okay. Here's a question. Why me? Why does the formula work on me, but not on Nelson or Clayton? If the secret is drinking your own blood, then it should work on them, too."

"The formula only works if you have the talisman," he said. "Surely you read that in the translation."

"I don't have a talisman."

Tucker laughed. "Of course you do, Elizabeth. Don't you see? *You* are the talisman. It's been you all along."

I took a step backward, reeling from that tidbit of information. That's when Kevin cried out, then sank to the floor clutching his side in pain, his crossbow skittering across the linoleum.

I looked up, saw Renault's burned face, and screamed.

Chapter 34

Jenny's scream joined mine as Renault leaped toward me. "Get away from her!" Tucker shouted even as Clayton dove for Kevin's crossbow.

Renault tackled me, and we rolled over, banging against the bookshelves and sending Latin texts tumbling down on us.

My head slammed against something hard, and the world started doing that inside-out thing. In the doorway, I saw Clayton let loose with the crossbow. Renault jerked sideways, twisting so that I was in front of him. As if in slow motion, I saw the wooden arrow fly straight and true.

Clayton's eyes were wide with horror, and I knew without a doubt that he would never, ever intentionally kill me. Not even to be human again. Unintentionally, though . . .

That, I think he may have just done.

Chapter 35

"*No!*"

Even as the arrow flew from the crossbow, Mr. Tucker leaped across the room. In that split second, I realized how old a vampire he must be, because he moved with such speed that my eyes couldn't even follow him. All I knew was that suddenly *he* was in front of me. *Directly* in front of me.

As in, Mr. Tucker was about to take Clayton's arrow in the chest.

"The empress must not die!" he bellowed, and then he flinched as the arrow hit him.

For a moment, I thought that Clayton's shot had missed its mark. Then I watched as my Latin teacher—as my maker—dissolved into gray ash, the wooden arrow having gone straight through his heart.

"You?" Renault said, scrambling off me, his eyes wide. "You're the one?"

I matched him scramble for scramble, moving in the opposite direction. "The one? The one *what*?"

"Forgive me," he said, his voice low and his head down. "Please, forgive me." He backed up two more paces, and then he bowed—yes, *bowed*—before turning and racing from the room.

What the—?

But I didn't have time to worry about it, because I was too busy being blindsided by the bigger picture. Or, more accurately, being blindsided by my boyfriend. "Oh, God. Oh, God. Oh, God," he said, grabbing my shoulders and pulling me into a hard, painful hug. "I'm so sorry. I'm so, so sorry! I didn't mean to do that!"

I hugged him back. "It's all right. I'm okay. See?" I indicated my still-whole self. "I'm fine. You didn't get me."

"I didn't get Renault, either. I got Mr. Tucker. I don't know how, since he's above me. I guess it's because I wasn't aiming for him. I didn't mean it, Beth! You know I didn't."

"Yes, but—" I cut myself off, my mouth closing with a snap. I'd been so freaked by Renault's sudden weirdness that

I'd completely spaced on the bigger picture. The *hugely* bigger picture. The picture where I stayed a vampire for the rest of my life. Death. Whatever.

Oh. My. God. And then I said it out loud: "Oh. My. God." I looked at Clayton. "*I* didn't kill him. And I didn't ask you to do it for me. That means I can't be . . . I can't ever be . . . I'm going to be a vampire forever."

"I didn't mean to, Beth. It was an accident. I would never . . . well, you know." He drew in a breath and rubbed his hands over his face. "Now I'm stuck, too."

I looked at him and saw him looking right back at me. He *wasn't* stuck, of course. Not technically. Kill me, and he'd be fine. For that matter, I'd be over the vampire-for-all-eternity problem.

But Clayton wasn't going to do that. A few weeks ago, maybe I'd been unsure. I wasn't anymore.

He held me close, and I shut my eyes tight, wishing for a good cry. "It's okay, Beth," he said. "If we're stuck, at least we're stuck together."

Chapter 36

"What really gets me," Jenny said as we rehashed the whole conflict for the ninety-millionth time, "is the way Kevin got the heck out of there."

"Yeah," I said, looking down at my bedroom floor. Kevin had heard my conversation with Clayton, which made things a little awkward since the first time we'd come to blows he'd let me live only because I had a chance to be redeemed.

"He loves you," Jenny said. "That's why he didn't kill you."

"That's why he left," I said. "The jury's still out on whether or not he'll try to stake me."

"I'm not interested in what Kevin thinks or does," Clayton

said. "Unless he tries to kill you, of course, and then he'll piss me off. But the thing that did interest me was all that 'empress' stuff. What was up with that?"

"I don't know," I said. "You have to admit, Tucker was always a little freaky. And old, too. Maybe too many centuries does that to a vampire?" I looked at Clayton, wondering if we'd live so many centuries that our brains would end up fried, too.

Clayton leaned back in my desk chair, then pushed off, rolling across the battered wood floor toward me. "Maybe he was crazy," he said. "Or maybe he knew what he was talking about."

"Empress?" I repeated. "In what universe?"

"Vampire universe, maybe?" Jenny said, and I shot her a dirty look.

"It's freaky," Clayton said. "I'll grant you that. But maybe it's also true. You saw the way Renault left you alone. He practically genuflected his way out of the school."

"And you *can* go outside during the day," Jenny said. "It's not like that works on every vamp."

I nodded and swallowed, remembering the way Nelson had turned into a crispy critter and the way Clayton's hand had fried.

"Maybe you are vampire royalty," Clayton said.

"Oh, please. My mother's a litigator and my father's a doctor. I inherited my smarts from them, but not a royal bloodline."

"Maybe vamp royalty is different," Jenny said. "Maybe Mr. Tucker was a prince or something, and when he turned you into a vampire, that made you a princess."

"I don't think so," Clayton said, shaking his head. "I think he was some sort of bodyguard."

I kicked the edge of my bed. "I bet there wasn't even a state Latin competition. He probably wanted me to practice translating in case I hadn't made enough progress with the formula."

Clayton and Jenny stared at me. "Focus," Clayton said. "I'm thinking that's not a big-ticket item."

I stuck out my tongue at him. "It's one more weird thing in a scenario that keeps getting weirder and weirder." I couldn't be an *empress*. I wasn't even popular!

I shook off the thoughts, forcing myself to stay firmly planted in the realm of reality. "You guys should go," I said. "My dad will be here any minute. I don't want to explain why I've got friends over at three in the morning."

"You sure you're okay?" Clayton asked.

"I'm fine. Honest." That wasn't entirely true, but I didn't feel like dumping a whole big guilt thing on my boyfriend.

Turn into the whiny sort of girlfriend, and he may decide to dump me. Or have someone stake me.

I swallowed, not at all happy to be having morbid-o thoughts again, then stood up and ushered them toward the door. "Seriously," I said. "I'm fine. And apparently I'm safe. At least for a while. It's been a whole night of drama, I don't need it from my dad, too."

Jenny nodded, and Clayton leaned in for a short but sweet kiss. And then they were both out of there, and I was alone in my room, in the dark.

Welcome home, me.

The trouble, of course, was that it was almost three a.m. Vampire afternoon. Which meant that I was *so* not interested in sleeping. And yet I really needed to. Too much had happened, and there was too much weirdness going on. I couldn't think about it all—not yet.

An army of vampires who desperately wanted me dead—and then suddenly didn't.

A maker who kept himself hidden and secret—until the last possible minute when he sacrificed himself to save my life.

A vamp who'd sworn to take me out suddenly turning tail and running—*and* bowing to me in the process.

And my almost-date for the evening exiting stage left so that he wouldn't have to kill me either.

I hadn't had a day this weird since the test-grading machine had gone whacko and spit back an F on my freshman algebra midterm. *That* had been one big honking mistake. This, though . . . ?

I had a feeling this wasn't a mistake. This was real. Inexplicable, strange, freaky, and pretty much unnerving. But very much real.

And, apparently, not something I could ignore. I might not want to think about it, but want and action weren't exactly jelling at the moment.

Frustrated, I quit pacing and parked myself in my desk chair. I think best when I'm making lists, and so that's what I decided to do then.

I rolled to my computer, pulled up a document, and started typing:

1. *Vampire royalty?*
2. *"Empress?"*
3. *Research Mr. Tucker? How old? Where from?*
4. *Can Clayton go outside if he drinks my blood?*

That last one made me start tapping the end of my pencil against my teeth. This is why I like lists, because the question hadn't even occurred to me until I started typing. But once my fingers were on the keys, the ideas started to flow. And *this* idea seemed real reasonable. After all, if I was the talisman, wouldn't my blood work on the vamps I made, too? Since they had my blood as well?

It seemed like a perfectly reasonable theory, and I was pondering how we could safely test it, when I noticed the little mail icon on my toolbar. I clicked over and pulled up my e-mail, and after I'd sorted through all the spam, I was left with a single message from Cary at the lab, the subject line reading simply: *Results.*

I clicked on it right away, and skimmed the note. *I almost didn't send you this, but I figured you'd hound me for the results, and if I didn't give them to you, you'd find someone else in the lab to do your bidding. Don't worry, though. Your secret is safe with me.*

Uh-oh.

He must be talking about the fact that I'm a vampire? What other secret could my blood reveal?

I pondered that for a minute, trying to come up with some possibilities. Then I realized I was stalling, so I steeled myself and clicked on the attachment. A document opened immediately, showing the results of the DNA testing, including a lot of scientific mumbo jumbo that I could have figured out if I'd tried hard enough.

I didn't, though. Because I'd already noticed the little box at the bottom for the lab tech's notes. *Paternity negative*, it said. *Sample blood not from blood relatives.*

I stared at the screen, the words practically burning into my brain. *Paternity negative.*

Paternity *negative*?

What the heck did that mean?

Just then, I heard a key rattle in the kitchen door, followed by the sound of my dad's briefcase dropping onto the table. Except he wasn't my dad after all. Paternity negative, right?

I had no idea who my real father was. More important, I had no idea who *I* was. A vampire empress? Or plain old Beth Frasier, undead valedictorian-to-be?

I didn't know, but I had a feeling I was going to find out.

Hopefully, though, the drama would wait until after I nailed my midterms . . .

Go back to school in style
with Berkley Jam

Girls That Growl (Available October 2007)
by Mari Mancusi
Third in this hip, sassy vampire series.

Demon Envy (Available October 2007)
by Erin Lynn
Being a teenager can be hell—especially if you're friends
with someone who was born there.

Queen Geeks in Love (Available November 2007)
by Laura Preble
"Give the nerd in you a chance to get up and shout" (*Girls'
Life* magazine) with the second book in this fresh series.

The Band: Finding Love (Available November 2007)
by Debra Garfinkle
Catch up with the hit band Amber Road as they navigate
their newfound fame—and their fragile emotions.

Manderley Prep: A BFF Novel (Available December 2007)
by Carol Culver
Welcome to exclusive academy of Manderley Prep, where
the only thing harder than the classes is fitting in.

Go to penguin.com to order!